BORN TO TRACK

Reuben Cole - The Early Years Book 1

STUART G. YATES

Dedicated to little Moreneto, this was the first work I completed
after you'd left us on July 11th, 2020.
And for Libby, who loved you so very much.

PROLOGUE

I n the early part of the Twentieth Century, Reuben Cole, one-time army scout, known to the Indian Nations as 'He Who Comes' is nearing the end of his blood-soaked career. Hard, unrelenting years of effort and violence have taken their toll. No longer the man he was, his final case almost cost him his life. The reality is he is old and slow, and he now accepts this, albeit reluctantly, as so many ageing people do. Announcing his retirement to his long-suffering lover, she tells him a magazine writer has arrived at their home, eager to record Cole's career to an avid readership thirsty for tales of the 'wild west'. Hesitant at first, Cole agrees and relates the formative part of his career during which time he learnt about tracking and how to stay alive in the harsh, unforgiving landscape of the West.

As he himself told the magazine writer, 'What you have here is the story as I lived it. I was not present for everything that happened, and such scenes were told to me at a later time. But it is all true, every word of it.'

This is his story.

CHAPTER ONE

His mother is close to death. He knows this without being told. Doc Miller used to visit every other day but recently it is twice a day. Reuben, fourteen years of age, would sit in the corner and watch the comings and goings without speaking, never asking. There is no need. He sees everything in the lines on their faces and the ghastly shade of his mother's rice-paper skin. Also, in the way his father shuffles around the house looking old and bent, barely able to meet his son's gaze.

Doc Miller squeezes his shoulder and gives him a reassuring nod. Reuben holds the old man's stare. "Will she get better?"

The Doc presses his lips together and shakes his head.

He steps away, leaving Reuben to his thoughts.

Reuben sinks deep within himself, turning his mind to memories and he puts his face in his hands and quietly weeps. She is his mother, and she is going to die. It is like his entire world is collapsing and he is helpless to prevent it.

On this morning, when he finally goes downstairs, the men stand in the parlour, glasses in their hands, none willing to meet his stare, so he decides to go out. He feels torn. His mother lies in her bed, and no one is with her. He should stay, stroke her fevered brow, but Doc Miller has warned him. He must not touch her. He even said it would be best to not even go in the same room as her. Taking that advice, throughout every day, Reuben would crouch in the hallway outside, head against the door, listening to her ragged breathing. But following advice does not take away the pain or the guilt. Now, with heavy treads, he slips out of the house, not knowing or caring if anyone sees him leave.

Outside, it is cold. Snow has already fallen in the night and, in the heavy whiteness of the sky, more threatens. He cares not. He mounts old Nora and takes her far away from the ranch. He loves the ranch. He loves the way the breeze moves through the fields, the way the sky stretches on forever, the distant mountains a purple smudge against the blue backdrop. Everything he sees is owned by his father and one day everything will belong to him. Reuben Cole. A boy whose future is guaranteed.

Except he doesn't want it.

He doesn't believe he wants to be a rancher. Not yet, not with his mother about to leave him forever. No more will he listen to her kind words, her guidance and encouragement. She is leaving him with his whole life still ahead of him, with all its uncertainties, excitement, adventure, and adversity, all for him to encounter alone.

So, he rides. His mind is a windswept landscape of constantly changing emotions, his fears tinged with sadness, mingling with dreams of the unknown. The big wide world is all around him and he finds it breathtaking but so daunting. So unpredictable.

He rides with his mind far away until the memories loom large and vivid. He recalls his mother's smiling face, her perfume filling his nostrils. If he closes his eyes, he can see her again. How she used to be before the sickness ravaged her features, made her stick thin and sallow-skinned. Beautiful. Smiling, forever smiling.

He reaches a place he does not know. Snapping himself from his reverie, he takes in the landscape. Around him, jagged, wind-scarred cliffs soar, so high he cannot see their summits. Birds fly there, no doubt buzzards eager for a feast. He shudders, twists, unhooks his canteen, and takes a long drink. Nora is breathing hard. They must have been riding for hours and often the snowdrifts were deep. He chides himself for not concentrating more on where he was heading.

He steers her towards a tangle of trees and gorse, and dismounts. He strokes the old mare along the neck and, working quickly, he unbuckles the saddle and relieves her of it. Pressing his face against her muzzle, he kisses her flared nostrils, and she responds, nickering softly.

Leading Nora amongst the overhanging branches, he puts down the saddle and loosening his pants, relieves himself against an outcrop of rock, closing his eyes to luxuriate in the feeling of relief. Nora snorts in disgust at the stench. He has held the contents of his bladder for too long.

There is hardtack in one of his bags. He takes a bite, clamps his teeth around it, munches until he can swallow. It tastes like old, dry rope, and he washes it down with water from his canteen. His father sometimes would bring whisky or rye with him to drink on longer rides. Reuben has yet to experience whisky. He wishes he had.

Returning to the shade, he puts a blanket over Nora's back before stretching himself out on the ground. The second blanket he puts around his shoulders. Although many small rocks jab into his back, he is tired, the day mild thanks to the sun and soon his eyes grow heavy. Within moments he is asleep.

Something forces him awake. A distant cry jerks him bolt upright. For a moment he is disorientated. Rubbing his eyes, he looks around. Nora stands still, her ears pricked. The sound comes again. Sharp shouts, too far away to recognise individual words, but close enough for Reuben to know these are the voices of several, angry men.

He gets up, throws off the blanket and shakes himself. Moving to where he put down the saddlebags, he pulls the squirrel gun from its sheath. It is an old gun given to him some years before by Floyd Henderson, one of the boss ranch hands. Proving himself something of a natural, Reuben would often take himself to higher ground, draw a bead on the main barn, and shoot the rats as they scurried to and fro. Henderson said he was a 'dead-eye shot', whatever that meant, but he basked in the big man's praise. He never expects to use the gun in anger. A tremor runs through him.

Darting from his shady spot, he crosses to an outcrop of rocks and settles himself down to watch.

Across the rugged terrain, there comes a man running. He is half-naked, long black hair trailing behind him like a horsetail. His pants are made from rough cloth, possibly animal hide and in his hand is a bow. Reuben sucks in air. An Indian. Henderson told him once that Kiowa hunt close by and if ever he saw any he was to tell his folks straight away. Savages are what Henderson calls them, but Reuben has never laid eyes on one, until now and, from where he squats, the man does not look very savage at all.

He is running with an easy grace across the snow, his long stride relaxed, his head still as if he is in deep concentration.

Given what is looming up behind him, this could well be the case.

There is a rider, using his hat to beat his horse's rump, urging the animal on. It is not this man who is shouting however and Reuben strains to see if he can catch anyone else out there on the plain.

There is no one within sight so he returns to watching.

The rider is gaining on the Indian. The ground underneath the snow is treacherous, broken by rocks, large and small, strewn all about, any of which could prove hazardous for the horse. Its canter is awkward, the animal taking care, but the rider appears oblivious, "Come on you paltry good-for-nothing!" But the horse is not stupid, and Reuben cannot help but laugh.

His amusement immediately leaves him when he sees the rider drawing his pistol. Several shots ring out, none of them hitting their target, and Reuben sees the Indian increase his run. He swerves from side to side in a ragged, unpredictable way. Reuben understands this is a way to disrupt the rider's aim. And he wonders, as he watches, why the savage does not stop, turn, and fire the bow.

As he focuses in, he sees why. The savage has no arrows.

He then sees a most remarkable thing.

The Indian does stop. He turns and waits, arms dangling by his side. Has he given up, thinks Reuben? Has he accepted his fate, resigning himself to the doom awaiting him?

But no. As the rider draws nearer, loosing off wild, inaccurate shots, the Indian moves at the last moment, swerving to one side, catching the reins, and pulling them down violently. The horse's head snaps to the side, a terrifying scream spouting from its foaming mouth. The rider lashes out with the revolver, now obviously empty but, like his shooting, this is ill-judged and the Indian grapples with his arm and swings him around in the saddle. Now all three, horse, rider and Indian, commence a macabre dance, as they move in a tight circle. The horse kicks up great plumes of powdered snow and the rider tries desperately to release himself. The Indian manages, at last, to pull the rider from the horse, which off-balance and terrified, keels over. The Indian leaps backwards to avoid the maelstrom of human and animal limbs as both crash into the dirt.

The hapless rider, caught beneath the bulk of his mount, struggles frantically. The Indian moves nimbly, the knife appearing from nowhere in his hand. The stricken rider holds out a palm, his voice, when he speaks, brittle with fear. "Please," he says, "please, no!" But the Indian ignores the man's desperate pleas. Swift and decisive, he plunges the heavy blade into the rider's flesh, slicing through his throat. An eruption of thick black blood follows but if this is to be the end then everyone is wrong.

From out of the white, frosted air, more riders appear, galloping forward, whooping with rage, guns drawn. Their shots go wide but, as they draw closer, it will not be long before the decreasing range will result in the Indian being hit. Reuben, who crouches low, locks his eyes on the unsettling scene enacting before him. He is torn between intervening and remaining as an impassive observer. The stories of these Indians, the horrors they have perpetrated, run through his mind. But something, the injustice of what he sees, causes him to react. He swings up his rifle, meaning to frighten the horses with a well-placed shot between their hooves and force them to veer away. This could give the Indian a chance to run or stand and make a fair fight of it.

Reuben is good with his rifle.

Squirrels move fast and he can hit them from a hundred paces, sometimes more. And a horse, it is so much bigger. A few evenly spaced shots in the ground between the animals' hooves will spook them, throw the riders perhaps, at the very least cause confusion.

He squints down the barrel, pulls in a breath, measures himself and eases off a shot.

He often looks back at that moment. In quiet times, alone in his bed, the early hours so black, so full of terror, he relives every detail as if he were there again. And each time the horror never diminishes.

The first shot hits the ground inches ahead of the lead horse. Exactly as he hopes, the horse screams, rears up, and throws the rider clean out of the saddle. Reuben does not need to check to know that the man hits the ground headfirst with such force that his neck breaks. Worse swiftly follows. As the man's body slams into hard, impacted earth, the gun still held in his hand goes off. Whether it is the angle or simply sheer fate, Reuben can only guess. Whatever the reason, the misplaced shot hits the rider following in the chest and he too falls.

The man writhes for a few moments before he grows rigid, one frozen arm extended upwards as if grasping for some invisible means of help.

There is none.

Two dead men in the space of a couple of dozen seconds.

The surviving riders battle to control horses wild with terror. They turn away and, spurring their mounts' flanks and whipping them with their reins, they gallop off in a billowing cloud of snow and a good deal of fear.

Standing watching, Reuben tries but finds he cannot move. Rooted to the spot in abject horror, he sees the two riderless horses bucking and kicking as they disappear into the distance, leaving the dead men on the ground.

The rifle slips from Reuben's fingers. He does not react. His mouth hangs open, his eyes unblinking, trying to come to terms with what he has done. For it is all down to him. His responsibility, his blind stupidity in arriving at a plan so ill-thought-out it could only ever result in disaster. He wishes he could run, but he has no strength.

And then something unheard and unseen presses against his back. A strong hand grips him under the chin as another holds a heavy-bladed knife against his throat.

Reuben feels his stomach lurch.

It is the Indian. He has sneaked up behind and is now about to kill him.

All strength leaves Reuben's legs and he buckles. But the man's hand slips from his throat grip him under his armpit and holds him up.

Pressing against his ear, a thickly accented voice says, "Don't faint on me, boy."

He turns Reuben around and stares. Reuben is drawn into those eyes, hypnotised by the moment, the danger. He wants to beg, to plead for his life, to make this savage understand but even though he forms the words in his mind, nothing escapes from his lips. It is as if he has lost the power to speak. He is at this man's mercy.

"Why did you help me?"

The question deserves an answer. Reuben knows this and yet he can conjure up no explanation. He is fearful that the savage will lose patience, strike him, beat him to the ground.

"Are you mute?" The Indian tilts his head. "Do not be afraid. You saved my life. I am not about to harm you. But if you are mute ... Give me a sign."

This savage is no idiot, no bumbling simpleton, but a thinker, a man who comprehends.

Reuben clears his throat, a huge effort as he believes any sort of movement or reaction will galvanise the savage into action. So, he waits and slowly his lips part. "I didn't ... I didn't mean to kill anyone."

"I am certain of that my young friend. But you have. That will mean they will come back. More of them. They will come back, and they will hunt us down, the both of us. So, we must leave this place, cut across country, and find somewhere to hole up. I cannot return to my village – to do so would bring danger to the women and children there. So, we must go, alone. Pick up your rifle and run with me. My name is Brown Bear."

"I'm Reuben. Reuben Cole."

"So then, Reuben. We must go."

"I have Nora. We could both ride her."

"That nag?"

"She may be old, but she is game."

"I trust you. I have little choice. You have given me the gift of life."

Reuben takes Nora and gingerly lifts himself into the saddle. He reaches out an arm and lifts his new friend to sit behind him. Reuben is young. Fear and uncertainty force him on. He silently prays that something similar will keep the strength in Nora's tired legs.

CHAPTER TWO

They ride at a steady pace, Reuben mindful of Nora's age. She is still strong, but she labours under the weight of two riders. So, Reuben treats her gently, never urging her on when she sometimes falters. Even so, they cover a good distance before Brown Bear, twisting around to look into the distance behind them, hisses. "I see signs of riders in pursuit."

Without a word, Reuben veers off to the left and heads towards a large cluster of rocks. Some are huge and are too big to climb, others offer them sufficient cover to hide, however, and Reuben heads for these. After dismounting, he takes Nora well out of sight. He hobbles her, aware that any surprises could spook her and force her to run off.

"You do that as if you are used to it," says the Indian. He is settling himself behind a large boulder and he mimes nocking an arrow. He does not have any and, as if to give weight to this fact, he shakes his head and turns his mouth down in serious contemplation. "If it comes to a fight, we will not prevail. You with your single-shot squirrel gun and me ... not one arrow."

"Our best bet is to stay hidden. Still and quiet, until they pass. We could then double-back, confuse them by scattering our tracks."

The Indian gazes wide-eyed at Reuben and shakes his head. "How old are you?"

"Almost fifteen."

"You speak with the mind of someone twice that age. I am glad we met."

"You'll forgive me if I hesitate in sharing that thought."

The Indian sniggers before he chances a look from the boulder behind which they both shelter. "They are moving to the east. Trackers they are not."

Now it is Reuben's turn to snigger. "You sound like a white man the way you talk."

"I have lived with your people for many years. I have tracked for the army now and then, made enough money to trade for food and equipment to help my family."

"You tracked for the army? When was that?"

"Some years ago. Things are changing as people think less of Indian attacks and more of the threat of fighting each other."

"I've heard there are arguments between some of the states and the government. I don't know much, only what Pa tells me. He says he ain't concerned as he doubts that if the fighting comes it will not spread out here."

"He could be right. I hope so."

"You think it will be bad if fighting does happen?"

"I think it will be very bad." He dips behind the boulder once again and stretches out his legs. "We should wait until dusk then go back the way we came." He winks. "As you suggested, my wise friend."

Reuben blows out a sigh. "We could try and make it back to my family's ranch. No one will think of going there."

"That may not be such a good idea."

"Why's that? Because you're an Indian?"

"They would prefer the word savage, I am sure."

"Then you'd be wrong. Pa fought in the Mexican War. He told me he learned a lot about mutual respect and tolerance during those times."

"And those lessons he has passed onto you."

"I like to think so."

"I know it, young friend." He tips his hat over his eyes and settles down.

Reuben watches him for some time before he too lies back, closes his eyes, and drifts off to sleep.

It is the morning of the funeral. Everyone who is anyone is there, with Pa looking like he's been frozen solid he's so rigid. Doc Miller is close, his face lined with worry, and Henderson too, the eternal cheroot clamped in the corner of his mouth. Henderson is wearing a gun and I wonder about that. Why is he wearing a gun on such a day, at Ma's funeral? Daisy our cook is also there, crying ceaselessly with her husband, Rolles, holding her tight. Rolles is an enormous man. He carries out all the household duties, cleaning, repairing, whatever Pa tells him to. I ain't ever heard him complain, but then again, I hardly ever hear him speak at all. Today is no exception except his facial features are scrunched up in sorrow.

Then there is Benny Bean. I'm not sure if that is his real name but that is what I call him on account he is tall and thin, like a bean. I do believe, however, his first name *is* Benny. He visited Ma every day when she was in her sickbed, and I recall he used to visit her before then, mostly when Pa was out on the range. That didn't bother me then because I didn't rightly know what it meant, but I'm older now, and I'm beginning to see things a lot more clearly than I used to. Benny is more upset than anyone, even Daisy. The tears are rolling unchecked down his face. He is wearing a black frock coat and striped trousers tucked into high black riding boots. He sports a thin, shoelace tie and a white dress shirt. He is clutching the black hat that would normally sit upon his head, a head topped with iron-grey hair. If anyone was to wonder who he was they would probably say he was the undertaker. But he ain't. He's my Ma's lover. I know that now. If I'd have known it before, I'm not sure what I would have done. Ma was always happy in his company. She never was in Pa's.

But Pa is a good man. I can see the tears welling in his eyes as the preacher, a thin skeletal man by the name of Hotspur, comes to the end of his prayer. Someone somewhere groans and I search the faces to try and find who, but I can't. There are so many people here. Maybe a hundred. It's a cold day, thank the Lord, because out here exposed to the elements the way you is, the sun could crack open your head like an egg. Maybe God is on our side, although I have often doubted it. Especially now, with Ma going the way she did. Someone said it was scarlet fever, someone else said it was smallpox. Darned if I know. All I know is she is dead, and I guess it was a kind of punishment for how she was carrying on. Did Pa know about any of that, I wonder? I glance over to him. There is only me and Pa now, and Pa frightens me. The way he can be so distant. So cold. I don't think I can ever remember a time when he held me close, comforted me. Not like Ma, who was always there with that lovely, warm smile. A smile that endured, even after Benny came into her life.

There's a scuffle. A startled cry rings out. I look up, and Pa is grappling with Benny and they are crashing to the ground. I'm moving forward, and I see Henderson drawing his gun. More people shout and yell, the assembly dispersing. This is not how it should be. Not here, not now, with Ma not even in the ground.

"For God's sake, stop!"

I gasp. It is me shouting. My voice sounding so sharp, so angry, and everyone looks. Benny struggles to his feet, beating off the dust from his immaculately pressed coat. Then comes the click of Henderson's gun as the hammer is cocked. My eyes zoom into the barrel as it swallows up the entire earth it is so big. It's going to blow a huge hole through my life and end Benny's.

How could it come to this?

I scream 'No!' but I know it is too late and the great gun explodes.

———

Reuben sits up, the scream dying on his lips. Sweat-soaked he sees Brown Bear gathering together his things, the normality of the scene bringing Reuben fully awake. He pushes the horror of his nightmare to the back of his mind, stands, yawns, and stretches like a cat, moaning with the pleasure of it. Smacking his lips, he gratefully accepts Brown Bear's proffered water canteen. "You were dreaming."

"Yeah."

"Crying out. I did not know if I should wake you. Who is Benny Bean?"

Reuben shrugs. He doesn't want to get into any of that right now. He drinks, wipes his mouth with the back of his hand and forces a smile. "How long have we slept?"

"An hour, maybe two. You, a lot longer."

"What, you let me sleep on after you'd woken up?"

"You needed the rest." He cranes his neck to take in the sky. "It will be evening soon. A good time for us to move."

In silence they prepare their belongings, loading up Nora who looked with those huge, glistening brown eyes at Reuben as if saying, 'Please treat me gently, kind master.'

"What are you thinking about?" asks Brown Bear, a thin smile on his brown, deeply etched face.

"How animals never complain. They just get on with life." He shakes his head. "I wish I could be like that sometimes."

"Only sometimes?" He blows out a sigh and turns his face to the horizon. "How far to your ranch?"

"Half a day, but with Nora burdened with the two of us, maybe longer."

"It would be foolish to press her too hard."

"Given that, we should be there by late afternoon tomorrow, I reckon."

"Maybe your father will not welcome me."

"I've already told you – he is tolerant, understanding. He is a considerate man."

A smile. Brown Bear motions that Reuben should mount up and soon they are making their way across the vastness of the snow-dusted plain, lit only by the developing twinkling of the stars.

CHAPTER THREE

"They are good."

It is the still of the morning, the air crisp, not a sound from anywhere. They have ridden through the night and are now a mere hour or so from the ranch. Brown Bear is down on his knees, reading the signs in the earth. "They have moved in behind us."

During the course of the early hours, he has already begun to show Reuben how to read various signs. Elementary things but revelatory to Reuben who knew nothing about the meaning of a broken piece of bracken, a slight impression in the ground. Now, sitting astride his faithful Nora, Reuben feels his stomach pitch over as he loads up his squirrel gun while he studies Brown Bear's serious expression. The gun has an optimum range of twenty paces at best. He needs all of his nerve and skill if he is going to make every shot tell. He swallows hard. "How is that possible?"

"Someone amongst their group is a tracker." He stands up, presses his hands into the small of his back and stretches. "They will ambush us, perhaps from there." He points to a spread of gorse intermingled with glistening outcrops of rock. "I cannot see any other place from where they could launch an attack."

"How many of them?"

"Enough."

Reuben blows out a sigh. "So, what do we do?"

"We ride to the east. Maybe an hour or two away there is the river. If we can make it there, find somewhere to hide, we might have a chance. A slim chance, but better than out here in the open."

"But if they break cover and ride after us, they'll be upon us. Nora cannot outpace them. We'll be dead."

"We have no choice, young friend. We're dead either way."

"I know this land," said Reuben, clenching his jaw, "and before we get to the river there is old Ma Gracie's cabin. We can make a stand in there."

"How far?"

"Difficult to say with certainty, but closer than anything else."

"Will she help?"

"Who? Ma Gracie?" Reuben chuckles despite the situation. "She passed away during the Revolution, so Pa told me! Her cabin is a ruin, with no roof. It'll probably be full of coyotes or racoons but it's the best we can do. But I think we should walk, not make out we know they are waiting for us. They could be watching, and they'll see the dust that Nora will kick up if she gallops."

"You're wiser than your years, my friend. If we make it through this, I will teach you every skill I know, from surviving out here in the wilderness to tracking your enemies. Or even your friends!"

That would be a good thing to know, thinks Reuben as he drops from the saddle, strokes Nora's nose, and takes the reins in his hand. "Thank you," he says and slowly starts the journey across the open ground towards Old Ma Gracie's cabin.

Neither dares to look towards where the gorse and boulders stand so grim and silent. They both know what awaits them there. Reuben could see no sign of them, but he trusts his Indian friend. Setting his gaze towards the new route he has chosen his pace is steady and his voice low as he speaks. "Tell me, Brown Bear, what is your tribe."

"My tribe?"

"I'm sorry, is that an offensive thing to ask? I've never ... Sorry, my experience in life does not extend to knowing much about Indians."

"My *people* you would call Shoshone. We live in small family groups and trade with white settlers to the northwest of here. It was during such a trade that the trouble first happened."

"Trouble with those men who were trying to kill you?"

Brown Bear nods. "At first they seemed reasonable enough. I had buffalo skins and sinew and I was looking for corn and squash to trade. Usually, such things are a formality. Many of those I traded with were known to me and my visits were welcome. But this time things had changed. These men were different. The fort I always went to was no longer there. Well, the building was there, the walls, the towers, but the soldiers had gone. Left. I suppose they must have been called away because of what is happening east. They left behind an assembly of men who were confused, lost, abandoned. Desperate even. Men who were drifters; men who ignored the rules."

"Rules? Pa always told me there were no rules out here, and certainly not in the Territories."

"Not formal rules, more unspoken ones. The ones that had enabled our lives to continue unhurried and without danger. But these new men, because that is what they were, they had no *respect* for the accepted ways. Almost as soon as I arrived in the fort with my pack mule trailing behind me, they abused and scolded me. Calling me names that I had heard before, but never directed to me. Some of them called me a 'murdering Comanch' and I tried my best not to look or listen. But that grew more difficult when they rounded on me. Six of them. Hard men with black, hate-filled eyes. The world has changed, my young friend, and I do not think it will return to how it was for many, many years."

"But why would such men go to that fort? What were they doing there if they did not wish to trade with you?"

"I believe they were fleeing from the troubles developing back in their homeland. I have known many such men, cowards, desperados, men whose only allegiance is to their own greed. Where many see confusion and danger, others see opportunity. Those men, they were thieves. Within moments of my arrival, they drew their guns, pulled me from my horse, and took to stripping my mule of the buffalo skins. As I tried my best to prevent them, they hit me, first in the belly then across the back of my head. They kicked me as I lay on the ground, their heavy boots going deep and hard into my side. I knew I had little chance to stop any of it but when one of them took me by the throat and pulled me to my feet, I struck back. I connected with his groin and as he fell, I took his gun. I acted quickly and foolishly because even as I ordered them to step away, I knew there were too many of them. They laughed, mocking me, and at that moment all of my strength left me. I lowered my arm and one, the man you shot at I think, knocked away the gun then hit me such a blow on the side of my head that I felt I was descending into a horrible, swirling black pit. By the time I came round everything was gone."

"They'd stolen your skins, your trading goods?"

"Everything. Even my mule and horse."

"What did you do?"

"I waited until nightfall. They were drinking in a broken-down saloon. I could hear them, and others, laughing and singing, drunk on their whisky. I found my horse but my mule ... They had killed my mule. No doubt he had kicked out at them as they tried to unburden him. He was always feisty, and I had learned to treat him with caution. But now he lay there, his eyes wide open, the blood black around his head."

He fell into silence and Reuben studied him. This man's love for his animal ran deep, a fact which Reuben found not only touching but humbling. The idea of such a man being termed 'savage' would not be contemplated ever again, as far as he was concerned.

After some moments, Brown Bear pulled in a shaking breath. "The skins were gone, of course, but my blanket roll, quiver and bow were still there. I did not wait but climbed across my horse's back and gently led him away."

"But they caught up with you."

"Faster than I thought. They shot my horse from under me ... the rest you know."

"But they stole your goods! What right did they have to hunt you down like ... like I don't know what, because any animal has more grace and godliness than they appear to have?"

"Godliness? You believe in the Great Spirit, my friend?"

"Great Spirit? Not sure I know what that means."

"I think it means the same thing as your god."

Reuben didn't know what to think. Brown Bear's story brought it all back − the killing, accidental or not − of those men. He shuddered as the images flashed across his mind. He was fourteen years old, a killer of men. How was he ever supposed to move on from that?

CHAPTER FOUR

I was to find out much later that Pa was going out of his mind with worry over where I had got to.

As Brown Bear and I were tramping across the plains, Pa was pacing his study, twisting his old, battered leather gloves between his fingers with old Lance, the range boss, and Henderson, his personal assistant (I never did discover what that entailed him doing) looking on, munching the unlit cheroot that he never seemed to be without.

"He's been out before," Lance had said.

"Never all night long! He's fourteen."

"He's tough," Henderson had added.

"Tough or not, he's out there alone. Anything could have happened to him."

"So, what do you want us to do, boss?" Lance had asked.

"I can't leave Gwyneth. Not now with her being so ... so close to the end and all."

"I realise that." Lance took in a large breath, replacing his hat, smoothing out the brim. "I shall ride out with a couple of the boys. We know roughly the direction he took, and we'll soon pick up his trail. Try not to worry. We will bring him home."

Pa had fallen into his chair, staring into space, eyes wet with tears. "I appreciate this, Lance. This is a difficult time for us all."

"Probably the reason why the boy went out," Henderson added, rolling the cigar from one corner of his mouth to the other. "We all react in different ways."

Lance gave his head a slight incline and left, his spurs singing as he crossed the wooden floor.

"I'll beat his sorry ass when he's brought back," my pa said through gritted teeth. "To ride out at such a time ..."

"The boy doesn't know how to cope. Neither do you, Saul. You need to rest up, get some sleep if you can. Your nerves are shot to pieces."

"How am I supposed to sleep at a time like this?"

"Try. I'll go over to Doc Miller's, get you a powder or something."

"I don't need no damn powder; I need my wife and boy back."

"Even so, I'll go visit the doc. Take it easy until I get back."

Henderson had turned to go when Pa called out, "You think he'll be all right? There are Indians out there."

"Not so many. Comanch are moving further south."

"Arapaho. There is always Arapaho."

"Boss, please, try not to upset yourself too much. Lance said he'll bring him home and Lance is the best there is."

"I know but I'm worried. I heard Fort Defiance has been abandoned and there are groups of traders milling about with nothing to do 'cept cause trouble. They concern me even more than Arapaho."

"Lance'll take care of any trouble. If you like, I can ride over to Defiance, check it out."

"No, no, I need you here right now. Let's just wait an' see."

"That's the most sensible thing you've said in a while. I know it ain't easy, but it won't always be like this."

"Ever the optimist."

"More the realist, Saul."

And with that he went out to ride to Doc Miller's, leaving Pa with his thoughts and his concerns, most of which were caused by me!

CHAPTER FIVE

They come to a wide, shallow dip in the gently undulating land. A backdrop of dark trees seems to act as an impenetrable divide between the sparse, unforgiving plain and whatever lies beyond. It is not this that takes Reuben's attention. His eyes are drawn to the broken, blackened cabin, its roof caved in, its shuttered windows wide open and, on the sagging porch, a rotting old rocking chair. Ghosts mingle with the creeping weeds which have infested the tired timbers; ghosts of the past, of forgotten families, of a simple but fulfilling life amongst a land full of hope and promise. Of a life gone badly wrong. For this place has not been inhabited for generations and as they move closer, Reuben feels that familiar sense of foreboding developing inside.

They have walked far. Reuben's legs ache but now all is forgotten. "It don't look too friendly, does it."

Next to him, Brown Bear surveys the surroundings. "Those trees could hide a whole army."

"You think they do?"

"Maybe not right now." He forces a grin, stark white in his bronzed, deeply etched face. "Our enemy is behind us, young friend. They will have by now realised we are not moving into their ambush. I believe we will fare better here against an attack."

"But what can we do against them with only a squirrel gun to defend ourselves with?"

"I shall search the woods for something to make arrows." He pats the broad-bladed knife at his hip. "We do not have long but I will do my best. Meanwhile, you hide Nora amongst the trees and make whatever you can of the cabin's interior. Use anything you find to help in the fight to come." He stops and smiles. To Reuben, it looks like a warm smile of encouragement. "Try not to be afraid. If we do not do these things, they will kill us without missing a heartbeat."

Reuben knows this is the truth, but he still cannot quell the pounding of his heart, or the horrible nausea percolating around inside his guts. He wishes he was older, stronger. More than anything, he wishes he had brought Pa's brand-new Spencer repeating rifle. Pa had been so proud of it when it arrived, the courier so impressed as he stood and watched Pa pulling apart the packaging. Then the hushed silence. Pa picking it up and gazing upon it as if it were a newfound love. Which perhaps it was. He would go out and fire it every single morning. And now it sat in a cabinet in the main hall and Reuben longs to have it next to him. It would even up the odds.

Sighing, he moves to the cabin after first hobbling Nora and tying her to a tree some ten paces inside the wood. On reaching the rear of the old cabin, he turns and checks. Nora cannot be seen. He smiles. At least something has gone right.

Of Brown Bear, there is no sign. Like one of those ghosts Reuben had ruminated about, the Indian has drifted away into thin air. He marvels at the man's ability to simply disappear. It also frightens him.

At the doorway, he stops and squints into the murkiness. Even the sky, filtering in from the remnants of the rafters, can barely penetrate the gloom.

He can just about make out the chaos within. Smashed pieces of furniture are thrown haphazardly into every part of the main room; various pots and pans and broken crockery lie scattered in the gaps. The long-dead fireplace is alive with piles of ash, rotting leaves, and dried twigs, all of it writhing with beetles and a myriad of other insects and crawly things. The more he looks, the more he notices the floor, made from compacted earth, moves with an entire nation of creatures. This could never be a place to abide in, but for a place to defend it might do.

If it wasn't for the open roof of course.

He peers at the portions of blue managing to break through and thinks this would once have been a good and homely place. Long ago. Before the rigours of the frontier life sucked it dry of the dreams that had once spurred people to come and settle in this part of the world. Their courage and fortitude, thinks Reuben, is something to admire. Those qualities are what he hopes come to him over the course of the next few hours.

Pushing aside his many conflicting thoughts, he begins to shape together a defensive ring, blocking up the two open windows flanking the door with sticks of old wood. He leaves sufficient gaps through which he can train his rifle. Then, for the door itself, he stacks whatever pieces of furniture that are large enough into the space. The door has long gone. The open entrance will be, apart from the roof, the main weakness of the defences.

There is another door, however, in the far wall. It may, so Reuben believes, lead to a bedroom. Before closing up the doorway completely so that Brown Bear can enter, Reuben moves to the closed door and pushes it open.

The ancient hinges creak and groan but at last, it screeches inwards.

He stands and for a moment and cannot believe what he sees.

Then the nightmare coalesces into horrifying reality and he screams.

CHAPTER SIX

I learned later, much later as it happens, that Lance and two of the range-team rode into Fort Defiance around the same time Brown Bear and I did our best to prepare the cabin.

It was cold when they got there and the men were wrapped up, making it easier for them to mingle with the others wandering aimlessly around the fort's interior. There was an atmosphere of despair in the place, all direction and sense of purpose gone. A heavy mood settled over the fort, talk of coming war on everyone's lips. It was as if they had surrendered themselves to the inevitability that disaster was about to strike and change lives forever.

Lance sought out the one building that continued to thrive – the saloon. Although calling it a saloon was an exaggeration. Lance explained later how the counter consisted of two long boards, maybe old doors, laid across four barrels. There were plenty of bottles arranged on the wall behind the makeshift bar and a chipped mirror. Whoever ran the place had worked hard to make it appear as normal as possible. Men pressed tightly together, all of them quaffing their beer and whisky whilst in the corner a small band of fiddle players played a series of bright, Scottish reels. All in all, the ambience was congenial and, given the circumstances, surprising. Did they know something he did not, Lance wondered?

Ordering drinks for himself and his companions, Lance studied the many faces of those crammed into the room, all of them flushed with drink.

"You'd think they were celebrating."

Lance looked across to one of his companions, Nils Lofgren, who, like Lance, scanned the surroundings.

"Now the army has gone," said Lance, "they feel they've been let off the leash."

"It'll end in trouble."

"No doubt. I want you to circulate, try and find out anything about Reuben. See if anything unexpected or out of the ordinary has happened over the last day or so. We might be able to pick up something. A clue. Anything."

Nils doffed his hat and disappeared within the press of rowdiness surrounding them.

"What d'you want me to do, boss?"

Lance nodded at his second companion. "Take a wander around outside, Mitch. It's a big fort, lots of barrack rooms, stables, outhouses, and offices. You might pick up something. We'll leave within the hour whatever the outcome and pick up the trail."

"If we can."

"We will. Not sure that Reuben would come this way, but I reckon he must be close. If he's run into trouble this would be the logical place to head for. It's well known and I'm sure Reuben could find his way if he had to. He's sensible enough."

"What if it's Indians, boss?"

"His pa was concerned about that, but there have been no reports of trouble from Arapaho for a long time. Comanch have moved on and so will they, I reckon. Especially when the hostilities begin."

"You think it'll come to that?"

"The news coming out of Carolina seems to suggest it and together with Lincoln's strong words, I reckon it's a certainty."

"But Carolina ain't gonna be able to resist on its own."

"No." Lance stared into his whisky glass. "We're looking down the barrel of a loaded gun, Mitch. I think it's about to go off." He sighed and drained his drink. "Now go and see what you can find."

Mitch Knowles adjusted his gun belt and wandered outside. For a few moments, Lance watched the man's retreating back before swinging around to the counter.

After a few more drinks, the three men met up outside in the dusty parade square. The squat, sun-bleached buildings pressed in around them on four sides. Despite the continuing rowdiness seeping out from the saloon an atmosphere of loneliness permeated from every mud-brick wall.

Lance wandered across to where the horses were hitched against a sagging rail. "Anything?"

"There was an incident," said Mitch, "but nothing to do with Reuben though."

"How d'you know?"

"Had something to do with an Indian."

"That's what I picked up," said Nils. "Seems like this Indian came in with some skins and got into a tussle with a group of drifters. They took exception, beat the hell out of him then shot his mule."

"Shot his mule? Why would they do that?"

Nils shrugged. "Sport, I guess. You know the type, Lance. Mean, bored, looking to make a quick buck whenever they can. They don't give a whole lot for anyone or anything, 'cepting themselves."

"Did they kill the Indian?"

"Nope. Seems like he ran off and they took after him."

"And that's it?"

Nils shrugged and rolled himself a cigarette using the tobacco from the pouch he carried at his waist. "No one said anything about anything else, Lance. This is the back of beyond and that's no doubt."

"That's about the sum of it," put in Mitch. "It might be an idea to follow the Indian. If he is heading across country, there might be a chance he could meet up with Reuben."

"And those chancers racing up behind? Is that what you think, Mitch?"

"It's all we got, Lance."

"If what you're saying is true then young Reuben is in a whole ocean of trouble."

"Could be."

"Then we ride. And we ride now."

CHAPTER SEVEN

Reuben takes the canteen and drinks fitfully.

"I ain't ever seen anything like this," Reuben says, and he gasps as he pulls the canteen from his lips.

Brown Bear stands in the bedroom doorway, unable to speak for a few moments.

A woman, who may or may not have been young once, sits on a rickety bed that almost fills the room, her back to the headboard, eyes wide and lifeless. Her filthy, ragged dress is covered in dry, black blood. In the centre of her chest is a gaping hole.

She has been dead for so long there no longer remains any smell of putrefaction. Skin the consistency of wax, mouth drawn tight, fingers extended as if in the last moments of supplication, the knuckles knotted like hard rope. Whoever has committed this ghastly deed left her in the throes of agony long ago, to bleed out alone.

"We'll have to bury her," Reuben says.

"We cannot."

"We *cannot*? I don't know anything about your beliefs or religion, or if you even have one, but we cannot leave her like this without burying her and—"

Brown Bear brushes past him and stands still. He listens, head tilted slightly to one side, a single raised hand stopping Reuben from continuing.

"What is it?"

Brown Bear flaps his hand, urging the young Reuben to stop talking. Reuben strains to hear but there is nothing.

"They are coming," says the Indian and reaches out for his bow. He has fashioned several arrows from what he has found amongst the trees. The points are sharpened with his knife, the ends bristling with feathers. The shafts may not be flawlessly straight, but he seems satisfied with them. His eyes narrow as he looks at his younger companion. "You remain here. Hide, keep still. Only shoot when you are certain of hitting your target."

Reuben feels his stomach pitch over. "But ... You ... Where will you be?"

"I will stay out of sight, to strike them from the side, cause them confusion and fear. They will panic, make mistakes. It is our only chance. There are six of them."

"How do you know that?"

"I have counted their horses."

Before Cole asks for further explanation, Brown Bear pads silently across the broken ground, disappearing between the trees. It is as if he were never there, a ghost.

Reuben is alone, the only sound that of his breathing.

He needs to run, to not stop running until he is home. He does not care if his pa rages, strikes out. He knows this will happen. He will climb the stairs and kneel beside his mother's bed again, imagine her chest rising and falling like rusty nails rattling in a tin bucket. Her skin glistening with sweat. Her lips stretched tight, blue, fluttering. She may see him. He does not know.

Anything even though it is all a dream. A wish.

Anything other than here and now, waiting for the men to come. Killers.

He sniffs loudly and runs the back of his hand across his nose. He is cold. He wishes he had a coat, but he never thought he would be this long away from home. Why did he ever leave? Stupid. Stupid idea. Stupid beyond belief.

There is the loud snap of a twig. A horse neighs. Reuben looks around wildly and sees nothing. He scurries back inside and whips up his squirrel gun. It is loaded, which is a godsend because his hands shake uncontrollably, and he knows he could not ram in the single ball down the barrel. Powder. He has powder. But does he have the strength? Is he brave enough? Shooting the man before, that was sheer luck. Or bad luck more like it. But nothing he planned to do. This, this is a whole new endeavour. Planned. Is he up to it?

They are drawing closer. He pulls across the upturned table and blocks the doorway. He crouches and remembers what is in the small bedroom behind him. The dead woman. The murdered woman.

Another shudder. He huddles behind the table and cradles the gun. He closes his eyes and tries so hard to control his breathing. Perhaps they will pass by. Perhaps this is nothing but a dream. A terrible nightmare that—

"Hey Brady, you take Tims and Coltrane round the back. Wyler, you hold the horses here. Billy-Joe, you take a look-see inside."

"*Me?* Why in the hell don't you go inside, Banner?"

"I'll be right behind you, Billy-Joe so don't go all blubbery on me, not now."

"I ain't going all blubbery, I'm just askin' you why you can't—"

"And I told you why, now do it before I lose my patience with you."

Reuben's heart pounds in his throat and ears. He is thirsty, confused, uncertain of what to do. Should he stay quiet, or stand, shoot this Billy-Joe as he steps up to the porch. He does not know, and the indecision renders him immobile. He sits, quaking. He knows his life clock, barely started, is running down to its close.

CHAPTER EIGHT

I heard this from Brown Bear much later. It is how he saw it and I have no way to confirm or reject it but what I do know is we are alive. And it is because of him.

Three dismounted men came stomping through the woods, making more noise than rampant buffalo. In their arrogance, they must have believed no one was there or, if there was, nothing would happen. Their plan, as much as could be understood by this careless, dismissive marching, was to circle the back of the old cabin, assess any danger, then assault from the rear. Perhaps to climb across the roof, drop into the interior through the gaping holes, despatch whoever was inside. They must have believed their quarry was there, quivering with fear, limbs frozen in terror, unable to respond.

They were wrong.

An arrow hit the lead man in the throat. For one horrible second everything stopped, the sheer shock of the attack incomprehensible to all those who saw. After a few seconds, the wounded man responded, gagging, desperately clawing at the shaft in a vain effort to pull it out. The blood froths over his hand and he crumples to his knees, eyes bulging with terror. Around him his companions break off, running in opposite directions, their guns blazing away, but it is doubtful whether the stricken man is aware of any of that. He folds forward, face slapping into the impacted ground and he does not move again.

Brown Bear is moving too. He does not wait to view the success of his first arrow. Unlike the others, he moves with the grace of a fallow deer, nimbly vaulting fallen trees, shadowing one of the others. He comes upon him in silence. The man is hastily feeding cap and ball into his pistol, but it is a lengthy process, and he reacts too late to the footfall behind him. The knife slices through his back, penetrating deep, cutting through his lungs. Soon he is flapping ineffectively. The blade withdraws and he falls. It strikes again, two, three times. Vicious, heartless blows, delivered with terrifying accuracy, destroying internal organs, engulfing the man's body in blood. He dies amongst the fallen leaves and scattered twigs and Brown Bear relieves the man of his gun before moving away to seek out another quarry.

Within moments he finds him. Sitting on a fallen tree, the man is feverishly reloading his pistol. He snaps his head up as Brown Bear appears from amongst the trees. He bleats like a newborn lamb calling for its mother. Stretching out his palms, he shakes his head, imploring, "Please, no, no!" But Brown Bear knows these men. Knows their type. They took everything from him, killed his mule, and now it is their turn to die.

He shoots the man, emptying the gun he holds until the man is nothing more than a mess of gaping wounds.

He throws away one gun and replaces it with the other. He quickly completes the reloading, takes more powder, cap and ball, and slinks back into the dark woods to make his way back to the cabin to give the boy a chance.

CHAPTER NINE

Reuben hears the sound of gunfire. It is surprisingly close, and he is gripped by uncertainty and fear. What does it mean? Brown Bear does not possess a gun. Could those men making their way through the woods have come across the Indian and killed him?

Reuben has no way of knowing, so he sits huddled behind the upturned table and waits.

He doesn't have to wait long.

There are more shots. Evenly spaced, not wild like before. It must mean only one thing – Brown Bear is shot. Dead. It is over.

And then he hears the urgent voices coming from outside.

"Billy-Joe, you stop stalling and get yerself into that cabin!"

"But that shooting is coming from the trees, Banner, hadn't we best check it out?"

"We will, just as soon as you've checked out that cabin. Now git!"

Sucking in a great breath, Reuben stands, the squirrel gun's stock in his shoulder, the thin long barrel aimed unerringly towards the lanky, yellow-haired man standing not half a dozen paces from him.

He cannot miss.

He doesn't.

The squirrel gun erupts, its single, small calibre ball striking the man in the throat, sending him flying backwards, arms wide as if in an attempt to keep himself upright. He hits the ground and writhes in agony, floundering in a desperate attempt to stop the flow of blood bubbling from the wound.

Reuben gapes at what he has done. The deliberate taking of another's life. His rifle falls from numb, quivering hands as the enormity of the act overcomes him.

Another, much older man stands a further ten paces or so beyond the dying man. He is staring in disbelief towards what has happened before his eyes look up and lock on Reuben's.

A tiny cry seeps from between the young man's lips as the man brings up his gun. He hears the slow, deliberate cocking of the hammer and closes his eyes in preparation for the inevitable.

But there is nothing but a suppressed whoosh of sound. Something cutting through the air and Reuben opens his eyes to see the man turning and running, waving his gun hand, and shouting towards yet another man struggling to control his horse, "Get the hell out, Wyler! There's too many of 'em!"

Reuben watches. The man called Wyler tries to turn his terrified horse away, in the meantime flapping his hand towards the other, urging him to move up away.

"Get mounted up, Banner! Quick, damn it. Quick!"

All the horses are nervous, the sound of the gunfire causing them to whinny and whine, out of control. Amidst the chaos of increasingly alarmed horseflesh, the man called Banner manages to avoid being kicked. He hauls himself onto the back of the nearest horse just as Brown Bear steps out from the trees to loose off another arrow. It strikes the first man, Wyler, high up on the left shoulder. He screams as he wrestles to control the horse beneath him. Banner spurs his mount on, takes Wyler's reins, and makes a bolt for it. Both of them gallop off, the left-behind horses in a frenzy, striking out in various directions, riderless, confused, and terrified.

Reuben, shaking, cannot find any words as the Indian comes before him, and all of a sudden, he is falling into his new friend's arms, all strength gone from his legs.

CHAPTER TEN

He cannot tell how long he has slept. If his unconscious state could be termed as such. It is a sleep unlike any other he has ever experienced. Full of stark, violent images. Of men, black with blood, screaming, begging for mercy, crying out to God for forgiveness, salvation, anything. And Reuben stands amongst a mass of writhing bodies, rifle held aloft, laughing at their suffering. But then as the blood runs unchecked down his arms to drip from rigid fingers, he is suddenly aware of his surroundings and he too takes up the cacophony of screams.

Someone is shaking him, and he awakes, alarmed, and sits up.

A man's face looms close and takes up the extent of his vision. A broad, flat face. Deeply etched, the flesh has the consistency of brown leather.

"Reuben, my friend, wake up!"

Reuben pushes the man's arms away and looks around, disorientated, frightened. "Where am I? Where's Pa? What's going on?"

He struggles to get to his feet but there is little strength left in his limbs and he collapses again, back hitting the large boulder behind him. He winces and grits his teeth to bite down the yelp coming up into his mouth.

"Reuben, you have a fever, I think. Brought on by the horrors you have witnessed."

The man is on his haunches and he looks concerned, a deep frown on his craggy face. Reuben thinks he knows him, but his mind is muddled, his senses reeling. Something gnaws away at his conscience. Something terrible has happened. "Oh my God ..."

"Do you know me? Do you know where you are?"

Around him, the vastness of the plain stretches in every direction. There is little cover out here, some clumps of sage, a few scatterings of rocks and scree, but essentially this is an endless, broad land which gives him no clues of his whereabouts. In the far distance, the purple smudge of mountains and above them the vastness of the sky, washed out, cloudless. "I'm nowhere near home."

"You are, my friend. I took you from the cabin and we have ridden in the direction of your father's ranch. We cannot be so very far, not now. We have ridden for perhaps three hours."

"Three hours ... I don't understand ..."

"You are shaken my young friend, and your memory is affected. It is understandable after what happened."

"Happened? Happened with what? I don't know what you're talking about. Help me up, will you?"

Reuben reaches out and grips the man's arms. They feel hard and strong beneath his fingers. The muscles flex and the man lifts him to his feet. Reuben stands, swaying slightly, and struggles to find his bearings. "Have I been hit? Injured in some way?"

"Not in the ways of the flesh, no. But in other ways, I think you have been. It will take some time to recollect but try not to think too much about that. The memories will return in their own time."

"What memories?" He drags his sleeve across his brow. "You're not making any sense. Where are we, damn it!" He rips himself free of the man's grip and stands and gawps. "Who are you? Why are you with me?"

"My friend." The man appears alarmed, his eyes alive with concern, perhaps even fear. "Can you not remember anything?"

Reuben whirls and lashes out at any number of invisible enemies that press all around. "Let me alone!"

And then the man takes hold of his shoulder, spins him about. "Quiet! Riders approach."

Reuben stumbles backwards. He hits the large rock and trips. Off-balance, senses out of control, he stumbles. From somewhere there is a loud cry, a voice from the depths of his memory. A voice he knows.

"Reuben!"

In great clouds of dust, men arrive, battling with horses which snort and stamp. Reuben is on his backside in the dirt. He looks through the mess of men, horses, and churned up earth to see one of the riders pistol-whipping the other man, the one with the brown face. The brown man goes down and a second man cracks the butt of his carbine across the side of the fallen man's head.

"Tie him up," roars the man that Reuben thinks he knows. He is a friendly-looking man, and he moves closer, hands out to help Reuben, a warm smile on his face. "Reuben," he says so softly, "it's all right, you're safe now. Let's go home."

CHAPTER ELEVEN

There is a strange, depressing atmosphere in the house. Reuben is in the doorway and there is Pa half-running towards him, the tears rolling down his face. He wraps his arms around his son and holds him close. "Oh, thank God you're safe," he says, his mouth pressed into Reuben's neck. "I thought I'd lost you."

Reuben does not understand this. He knows this building is his home despite not recognising any of its features. It is the sense of the place, the smell. Everything else is a vague, impenetrable fog.

"Come on, let's get you something to eat," says the man he knows is his father. "I'll get Isabelle to get a bath ready. You can relax."

As if in a sort of daze, not wholly aware of where he is going, hands gently lead him up the broad staircase. A woman, raven-haired, beautiful, is smiling. She takes his hand and leads him into a wide exquisitely furnished room. It smells of lavender and a single window looks out across the expanse of the ranch. Reuben moves to it as the woman says, "I will get a bath ready, Master Reuben."

But Reuben's attention is not on the woman or his surroundings. He knows there is something more important he needs to address. Something pressing, immediate.

From beyond the glass, he sees them taking the brown man. They have beaten him, and they drag him across the front yard, his naked feet trailing across the ground.

"We'll hang him," says his father from behind him. Reuben turns to see him standing, hands on hips, the smile no longer on his face, replaced by a terrifying grimace. "I don't know what the hell he did to you, boy, but as God is my witness, I shall not let this pass without retribution. He'll hang and we'll watch him die. I hope you can find some peace after that."

He leaves the room and Reuben does not have the words because nothing is making any sense. He turns again and looks through the window. They are lashing the brown man's wrists behind him with leather cords. He can barely stand. Again, they drag him, this time to a barn, and throw him inside. A tall man brings down the bar to secure the double doors. He dusts his gloved hands together and he is laughing, although Reuben cannot hear it. His companions are laughing too, and they move away and look proud. Proud of what they have achieved.

But what is it they have achieved, Reuben asks himself? He presses his forehead against the cold glass. There is something not right about this. He struggles to remember, but all he has are flickering, jagged scenes stuttering across his mind. There is gunfire. Lots of gunfire. And a man, blond-haired, skinny, he's eyes wide with surprise. And horror.

Then the boom of a single gunshot.

Reuben's eyes snap open. He is stunned, barely able to focus on the world beyond the glass. Gradually, his mind clears, the mist parting for him to make out reality, the world around him. Blowing out a sigh, he swings around. Pieces are dropping into place. Not all of them evenly, but he has the semblance of the truth, of what happened. He knows, with frightening certainty, he killed a man the day before. Stood up and shot him. Deliberately. No accident this time. He recalled that accident, the deaths of the two men and how he saved the Indian fleeing for his life.

Brown Bear. The brown man they are beating to death and are about to hang is his friend!

He races out of the room, bounding down the stairs carelessly, sliding over the last few steps to land on his knees. Winded, he ignores the pain and clambers to his feet just as his father emerges from his spacious drawing room with its fine collection of books and paintings. His inner sanctum. It protects him from the worries and fears that sweep through this house, the constant threat of death. Reuben's mother, always so close to death, holding on to a thin, fragile thread.

"Reuben? What are you doing? You need to rest."

Reuben sways but when his father steps closer, he holds up both hands. "No! Brown Bear, what do you think you are doing with him? You cannot—"

"Brown Bear? You mean that murderous savage who tried to kill you?"

"It was ... Dear God, Pa – he saved my life!"

"*What?* Are you insane? Lance caught him the act. Your brains are addled, all of it mixed up because of what happened to you!"

Reuben shakes, his body convulsing. He is fighting against an overwhelming desire to fall down, close his eyes and sleep for a hundred years. "No," he says, voice so small and frightened. "No, Pa. He *saved* me. The men who we fought? They were the ones. Pa, the ones coming after me for what I'd done." it is his turn to move forward. He places his hands upon his father's shoulders and stares deep into his eyes. "Pa, believe me. Without him, I'd be dead, and you'd be about to bury two of your family."

His father reels backwards, the words like slaps across his face. He blubbers, lips trembling. His voice is nothing more than a croak, "Reu ... ben..."

Without another word, Reuben barges past his father and runs outside. He ignores the cries behind him, the men by the fenced paddock in the centre and he runs, throws back the bar, breaks into the barn and there finds Brown Bear suspended from a roof beam. He runs to his friend. "Brown Bear, speak to me!"

The Indian, whose wrists are bleeding from where the leather cords bite into his wrists, looks down and the flicker of a smile crosses his broken, bruised face. "My friend ..."

"Hold on, hold on." Reuben whirls as a strong hand grips his shoulder. It is Lance, the range boss. He appears angry. "You cut him down, Lance. You cut him down and then you take him inside."

"I'll do no such thing – that savage is going to swing for what he did."

"He hasn't done *anything*. Did you shoot him?"

"Shoot him? Nah, that was just a little game, scaring the hell out of him. You seem a tad overly concerned about him, Reuben."

"He's my friend. Now cut him down. I order it."

"*You* order it?" It is Nils Lofgren, one of the men who has beaten Brown Bear to within an inch of his death. "He tried to murder you, you ignorant cub."

"No, he didn't. He saved me."

"We saw him," puts in Lance, "we saw him with you. Wrestling with you, about to put that knife into you!"

"No, no, no! You've got it all wrong."

"I don't think so. Nils, take Master Reuben inside until we get this done."

"*No!*"

Reuben knocks away Lance's hand from where it is still gripping his shoulder and, in the same movement, he grabs the range boss's gun and tugs it from the holster. He steps back, engaging the hammer. "Cut him down, or so help me I'll kill the lot of you."

"Reuben!"

Everyone turns to see Reuben's father as he strides across the yard to the barn entrance. He looks a dishevelled mess, the stress and anxiety of the last days all coming to the fore. He seems to be close to collapse. He sweats, he trembles. The tears roll down his face.

"Reuben, you put that gun down!"

"No, Pa. I've always followed you, listened to you and done your bidding, but not now." He turns his eyes again to Lance. "I'll not ask you again." And then, unbelievably, and perhaps most terrifying of all, he smiles. "And don't think I won't. I've killed three men over the last few days and I'll not hesitate in killing you."

Lance shoots a look towards Reuben's father who stands, beaten and afraid. He nods once.

Reuben steps away to give the men room to step closer. He watches them as they cut Brown Bear down, one of the men supporting the legs whilst Lance cuts through the leather binding the wrists.

When they are done and Brown Bear is on the ground, Reuben gestures with the gun. "Take him inside the house and tend to him."

"I'll thrash you for this," growls Lance as he steps away from Brown Bear's unconscious body.

"No, you won't," says Reuben. "I'm no longer a little boy, Lance, that you can bully and threaten. Those days are over."

"You'd put that filthy savage ahead of me?"

Lance's eyes are bulging, his face contorted and red as if seized by apoplexy.

"He's the man who saved my life," said Reuben. "He's my friend."

CHAPTER TWELVE

They sit around the large dining table, Reuben at one end, his father at the other. Both stare into their soup. A servant, a thin old Mexican known only as Miguel, stands and waits. There is a curious half-smile on his burnished face as if he is the keeper of amusing secrets. Reuben has always felt a bond with him. It is a bond similar to one he has developed with Brown Bear who sleeps in one of the upstairs bedrooms.

Finishing his soup, Reuben pushes the bowl away and sits back. Miguel steps away from the wall and takes the finished soup away.

"The men you killed...?" comes the voice from the far end of the table.

Reuben looks across to his father. He sits huddled, sunk inside himself. He appears like a small child, but then the table is large, more than twelve feet long. Is that the reason?

Reuben stares at his father. "I didn't mean to do it. It was a horrible accident, but they probably didn't see it that way. They came after us, Pa, and they would have killed us if Brown Bear hadn't stepped up."

"You seem to admire him."

"I learned a lot from him in the short time I was in his company. He's gonna teach me how to track."

"How to ...?" His father thrust himself backwards in his chair in exasperation, throwing down his spoon so that it splashed into the soup before bouncing sideways to crash to the floor. "Track? Are you mad, boy? *Track*? You don't need to do such things. We have charge hands and cowboys in abundance to carry out any such duties."

"I don't care what we have, Pa. I'm not gonna be a ranch hand."

"Of course you're not – you're going to be a ranch owner! When I'm gone, all of this will be yours."

"I'm not sure I want it." He ignored his father's outraged, gaping look and hurried on. "I'm happiest on my own, Pa, out on the range. I'm gonna join the army, scout for 'em."

His father's silence was worse than anything he could have prepared himself for. Miguel arrived with the next course, and Reuben stared down at the steak, green beans draped over it, the smell making his mouth drool.

"I can only say how relieved I am that your mother will not be here to see her only son become nothing more than an army lackey."

"Instead of a ranch lackey, you mean?"

"It's your birthright!"

"But it's not what I want."

A silence fell over them and it remained there for a long time.

He climbs the stairs, each one seeming to echo in its creaks the fear in his heart. For how many more days would he do this, to visit his ailing mother in her sickbed, sit beside her, hold her hands, and gaze at her as she struggled vainly against the inevitable? As he reaches the top, he pauses and strains to hear anything. One day, he knows he will do such a thing, and there will be nothing. A grim, horrible silence. She will have stopped breathing, and he would not have been with her. Gripped by a sudden terror of this thought becoming reality, he burst through her door.

There she lay, as always, propped up with pillows, her face shining with a thin film of perspiration, her pallor a sickly green, but she breathed. Reuben almost swoons with relief and he half-stumbles to her bedside and collapses into the little hard-backed chair next to her. This is where he always sits.

He reaches out and takes one cold, frail hand and squeezes it slightly. A tiny murmur and she turns her head to look at him. Her eyes wrinkle. A smile. This takes massive effort, but he knows she is pleased, and that is all that matters. A tiny flicker of normality in a world gone mad.

She does not speak. He talks, telling her something of his day, but not all of it. He does not want to cause her distress. Doc Miller said to let her rest. Reuben never quite understood the point of that. She was dying. One day soon she would be dead, and then she could rest. For now, he wanted her awake because even in her weakened state she was still his mother, and he loved her. More than anything.

He sits and he studies her face, the obvious discomfort there, but also her strength. How she manages to hold on is a wonder to him. It is something he hopes to develop himself. That strength of character, that well of resilience he managed to access when confronted with almost certain death back at the cabin. He is certain he has inherited such traits from his mother. What is he going to do without her?

Sometime later, he moves away. She is sleeping, her breathing shallow but not laboured as it usually is. He treads softly, crossing the room to the door. As his fingers curl around the handle, her voice comes to him, sounding strong. "Reuben…"

He turns, wide-eyed. Unable to believe she can be so coherent. "Yes, mama?"

"I love you, Reuben. You're my best boy."

Her eyes close. His eyes well up with tears.

They are the last words she ever speaks.

CHAPTER THIRTEEN

I am not here to tell stories of things I have no knowledge of, but what follows are the words of Lance, conveyed to me and my father around the dining room table. He has already told of his arrival at Fort Defiance, but now he regales us of what he discovered about the nature of the men who were to track me and Brown Bear down, all of which resulted in the firefight at the cabin.

Lance sat at the side of the dining table, elbows on the top, chin cupped in his hands. He slowly related what he had learned from questioning several drunks and gamblers in Fort Defiance. "It seems that the leader of a pretty sorry gang of chancers went by the name of Banner. He was not the sort of man to share a bed with, nor indeed anything with. A violent, uncaring man, he moved west after shooting dead a bank teller in a small New England town. Since then, he has wandered aimlessly from one pioneering town to the next until arriving at Fort Defiance. Penniless and looking for work and other 'opportunities' he fell in with a bad bunch. Spending almost all of their time in the fort saloon, they gambled and drank away their days until one of them spotted a lone Indian arriving at the fort with a mule laden down with buffalo skins. Accosting the Indian, they later reacted when the Indian managed to escape. They set after him and that was the last anyone heard of him."

"And these were the men who came after you?" asks Pa, his stern eyes boring into me.

I wasn't about to be intimidated. I sit up straight, returning his gaze. "I believe they must have been, Pa."

"But why come after you?"

At this point, Lance swivels in his seat so that he faces me square on. "That is the part I don't quite get."

"I think it's time for you to tell us everything, Reuben."

So, I do. I take a deep breath to settle myself and then relate everything that happened, from my riding out across the plains, to seeing Brown Bear being run down by those murdering scum, of my shot that led to so much violence and the final shootout at the cabin. I leave nothing out, being as honest and open as I can be. Both of them listen without comment. And when I finish, Pa is the first to react. He sits back, folds his arms and that look ... it is withering.

"You saved the life of a savage?"

This is Lance. His expression is different from Pa's. Where Pa's is serious, uncompromising, Lance's is full of bitterness, even disgust. His mouth is curled down as if he is savouring something bad.

I am not going to be browbeaten. I do not care what Lance thinks. He has lived his life out on the range, but I doubt he has ever conversed with a Native. That is how I like to refer to them as. I have read history. I have listened. They were here thousands of years before us. If anyone has a right to this land, it is them.

"I saved the life of a human being," I say, keeping my voice low. I do not wish to lose my temper with Lance. He is my father's most trusted associate, but his manner and his ideas are distasteful to me. I am almost fifteen years of age. My mind can still be moulded, but not in the way Lance would like.

Looking back is not easy. The passage of the years makes remembering difficult and so many things have happened to me in my life since those days that sometimes I forget the details. So, I am recalling events with an adult's eye, not the impetuosity of youth. But I do remember Lance and the expression clouding his features. He detested me. I could see it in every line, every wrinkle. I was too much like my mother, I could hear him thinking. Not enough like my father, the man who had built the ranch out of nothing all those years ago. Long before I was born, he and Lance worked the land, making it fertile, transforming dust and scrub into the gently rolling landscape over which horses and cattle could run and graze. For ten or more years they toiled, and success came slowly, but success *did* come, and the family spread blossomed, abundant with life. Lance and Henderson fought Arapaho and Comanche back in those days whilst Pa nursed my mother, who was always sickly. And when she fell pregnant with me, times were hard and dangerous. But they won through and my birth was celebrated. Soon, however, with the passing of the years, Lance more than anyone turned against me. He thought of me as weak, untrustworthy, a dreamer who would never give himself entirely to the ranch. In all of that, he was right, apart from the 'weak' part. I knew I was not weak, but my strength was different from his, and Pa's. I did not see my future on the back of a horse, driving cattle to market. I wanted to do something else. Give back. Serve.

So here I was.

At the table, holding Lance's raging gaze.

"I know what they are like, don't forget," he says through gritted teeth. "I've fought them, killed them. They are dishonest, vengeful, full of hate."

"A little like yourself, Lance?"

I see his hands grip the arms of his chair. Livid, barely able to control his anger, he half-rises out of his chair.

"*Lance,*" snaps Pa, "sit down and let it go."

"He's your blood, but I won't be insulted." He collapsed back into his seat, his face red, breathing erratic. "I haven't forgotten you pulled a gun on me, boy. I won't let that go unanswered."

"You forget," I say, and I can't help but smile, "that was your gun, Lance." And to make the point, I pat the butt of the pistol I have stuffed inside my waistband. "This gun."

"Are you gonna let him get away with this?" Lance spits, rounding on Pa who is also now beginning to rumble with anger.

"Reuben, you better back up. I want you and the savage out by mornin', you hear me. Take your bedroll and a couple of horses – not that nag you usually ride. A good, strong horse. You ride out and you make it right."

"How? By killing them?"

"There ain't no other course, boy. You brought this upon all our heads, and it is up to you to fix it."

"That's magnanimous of you, Pa."

Lance scoffs, "You'd be better spending more of your time learning how to rope steers than reading your fancy books."

He was right in that, I have to confess. Ma introduced me to reading when I could barely walk, and I'd never stopped. I didn't see it as an obstacle to growing up, rather the opposite. Locked inside the ranch, no matter how vast it may have been, reading gave me the keys to escape. I read, and I learned. Now, I yearned to experience for myself what lay beyond the boundaries of our land. Not in the way Lance and Pa were urging. On my own terms. Those men who were coming, as I knew they were, stood in my way.

"All right, Pa," I say. I stoop down and pick up the chair I threw down. I stare at it for a moment. "I'll make this right but, Lance, you stay out of my way from now on."

"Is that a threat?"

"Nope, it's a request."

"Polite of you."

I smirk and go to move away.

"Take some saddle guns," says Pa. "Don't take the Remington. There's a brace of Colt Dragoons in the hall that'll do better, together with my old Hall's carbine. You can take that with you, Reuben. It served me well and it'll do the job."

"You make sure you take enough cap and ball," puts in Lance.

"And powder," says Pa.

Keeping myself calm, I say, "Your concern is touching. The both of you."

I leave, hearing the curses forming on their lips.

Out of earshot, I make my way outside. Almost immediately, I see Brown Bear sitting in the shade. He looks up as I approach.

"Can you ride?" I ask him.

He frowns, gives a grunt. "We are going somewhere?"

"We're gonna find those others. The ones who got away."

"They will have found more friends, promising them the opportunity to make money."

"Yeah, by breaking in here and stealing all of Pa's treasure."

He gets to his feet and I see him wince. The cuts and bruises on his face are swollen, distorting his features.

"Are you sure you can ride?"

"I am sure. When do we leave?"

"First light. Pa's given me two horses and we have guns. Lots of guns."

"Then we must prepare, my friend. I do not think I am welcome here."

I give a small smile. "Me neither, my friend. Me neither."

CHAPTER FOURTEEN

The following day I awoke to find the weather crisp and dry, Brown Bear already waiting with the horses loaded up with provisions. We had decided to try and make our way back to the old cabin. I had not mentioned to anyone the body of the woman I'd found there. With everything that had passed since, I had not even talked about it with Brown Bear. It was a mystery. What had happened there? Murder, yes. But the reasons? There had to be some clues there, so I made up my mind to find out what they might be. Yes, it was a diversion, but that cabin was the centre of our life and death struggle with those men, so perhaps Brown Bear could pick up the trail of the survivors after we had searched the place.

On the way down to the dining room, I said good morning to Lucilla, one of the maids, and I saw there were tears in her eyes. I thought nothing of it. Lucilla was mute. A good, hard-working girl, we had always got on well and I assumed that perhaps she was upset at my leaving. But then I heard the pounding of footsteps racing up the main staircase, and I knew there was something else, something very terrible going on.

Big, lumbering Rolles came out from the kitchen, his eyes wide.

"Oh, Master Reuben," he said.

I froze. The realisation that the dreaded moment had finally come seemed to petrify me. I managed to turn my head to see Daisy, the cook, stumbling down the stairs, hands gripping the bannister. She was crying, and when she reached the bottom step, she collapsed. Rolles went to her. From out of the kitchen emerges Miguel, drawn and ashen. It seems the entire household is suffering from the news. And then Pa appeared at the top, white as death, shaking uncontrollably.

Everything and everyone was moving around me at lightning speed. It was as if I was a spectator to it all. Detached and distant, I saw people running backwards and forwards, lots of shouting, crying, flapping of arms, and wringing of hands.

Then, Doc Miller, jumping down from his buggy. I watched him through the wide-open doors as he runs inside, barely stopping to shoot me a glance, a glance that spoke volumes. He takes the steps two at a time.

Henderson strides to me. His face is dark. "I'm sorry, Reuben."

I frown. Although I realise what has happened, the shock of it hits me like a sledgehammer in the chest. I reel backwards, groping for something, anything to check my collapse. Rolles it is who catches me, his great arms lifting me as if I am a child. He takes me to a nearby couch and gently lays me down. I see him, and he is trembling. Henderson steps up beside him. "She took bad in the night," he says, his voice no longer that big, booming sound that I so often heard blasting out across the range. And then he did something I'd never seen before. He takes the cheroot from his mouth and stares at it, his eyes filled with sadness. "I raced over to get the doc but ... but I think maybe it's too late. I'm sorry."

I blink, shake my head, still not wholly aware of my surroundings, passing through everything as if in a dream. Miguel sits down beside me, and he reaches out and holds my hand. I collapse into his arms and he holds me so tightly.

It is then that Billy Bean erupts into the house. He is beside himself as if struck with a fever, the sweat glistening on his forehead, and he is sobbing like a child. He goes to move towards the staircase, but Henderson blocks his way, hand on his gun. "No, Billy, you won't be going up there today."

"You let me pass, damn you, or I swear I'll—"

I saw Rolles step in and land a swinging haymaker right into Bean's jaw, dumping him to the ground where he lay, unconscious.

"Get him out of here," growled Henderson and he turns away, and his eyes bore into mine. "There's a lot you don't know, Reuben. Maybe your pa will talk to you about it after ... after this is all done."

"Done and buried," I say in a quiet voice. I disentangle myself from Miguel's embrace and run the flat of one hand over my face. "I already know," I say. I can hear Henderson's gasp. Beside him, Rolles is taking Billy Bean outside. I shake my head. "I've known for a long time."

"I don't see how you could when we ourselves didn't even—"

I hold up a hand. "I'll tell you one day." I don't mean to sound so patronising, but I am sick of being treated like an ignorant kid by these people. Henderson has been with the family almost as long as Lance. Unlike Lance, he is not a chargehand, not in any true meaning of the word a cowboy. He is my father's bodyguard if you like. A man who uses his gun like a clerk uses a pen. Natural. That's what he is. A natural gunfighter. A killer. He used to frighten me when I was a kid, and Ma always used to whisper in my ear, "You be careful of that man, Reuben. Don't ever rile him."

I took her advice on board, never had crossed words with him, but now Ma was no longer here to give advice and the knowledge hit me and brought the tears to my eyes once more.

My life was never going to be the same again.

CHAPTER FIFTEEN

W e stood around the open grave, heads bowed, hands clasped in front in aspects of prayer. Daisy is crying and, beside her, the giant Rolles holds her close. Miguel is devastated. He loved my mother so. I study their faces, one by one. A little way off is Lance, with some of the cowboys, their hats off, scrunched up in leather-gloved hands. Doc Miller is also here. His face is streaked with tears and Henderson, ashen, his frock coat hanging open to reveal the pearl-handled Navy at his waist. I wonder about that and suddenly it hits me – this is my dream! I have experienced this all before, only in my dream, the difference is that Billy Bean was here. He is not here, in reality, thank God.

Reverend Small clears his throat and starts his eulogy. I don't hear it. My mind is elsewhere. In the far distance, Brown Bear is sitting under the shade of a tree. Our horses nibble at dry tufts next to him. Soon, we will be on our way, leaving all of this far behind. I'm not sure if I want to return now that Ma has left us. I stare down into that awful, black hole and see the top of her coffin. There is a single red rose lying on the lid. Who placed it there? I cannot think. Could it have been Pa? I doubt it because he has not even come. He sits in his library, sipping whisky, staring at the rows of his books, most of which he has never read. That was where I found him after Doc Miller declared Ma dead. I reeled at the word but Pa, his lips trembling, disappeared into his room, and he has not emerged since. That was yesterday. Now, Ma lies in the ground, and Pa drinks whisky. My hatred for him is building. No wonder Ma looked for affection elsewhere. In my dream, Pa stood devastated at the loss of his wife but that was my hopeful meandering thoughts. My wishes. In reality, my parents were never like that. There was no love, only resentment on both sides for a pair of lives wasted.

A sudden cry makes me lookup. Henderson is reacting too, and across the ground, a man is struggling with Lance and the others.

I gasp.

It is Billy Bean, arms lashing out in his pathetic struggle to free himself from Lance's hold.

"I want to see her," he shouts out.

I put a trembling hand against my mouth to prevent me from shouting out a reply. Although I try to understand his feelings, this is not his moment. It is mine and everyone else's, all those who have lived every day with Ma. Perhaps Billy has a right to pay his respects and say his goodbyes, but not now. Later, when we have returned to the house or, in my case, across the range.

Not now, Billy. Wait your turn.

Henderson, I know, doesn't see it that way. He is already striding across to where those men struggle.

I know what is going to happen. I have seen it in my dream.

But what I see is nothing like my dream.

In a wild, desperate flurry of movement, Billy Bean breaks free. He has a pistol. Whether it is his or not, I cannot say, but the pistol is drawn, and the hammer cocked. It is wavering in his hand as if it is too heavy for him to hold. Perhaps it is.

"I need to see her, you villains! Get out of my way."

"You hold your tongue," snaps Henderson. The others look at him and step away. Even Lance, who I have always thought a brute of a man, seems fearful.

Billy snarls, showing teeth gritted in a face livid with anger and sorrow, "I just want to see her."

"I know what it is you want," comes Henderson's reply. "You've already caused too much pain for this family, now get off this land before I have you horsewhipped."

But I could see it all playing out, even before it starts. Billy isn't going anywhere. I know he loved my mother, and she him. They have carried on their relationship in secret, but it is a secret everybody knows about, including Pa. Nobody has ever said anything, keeping their thoughts to themselves. As long as Ma lived, that was the way it continued, but now ... now anyone can speak their mind.

The shot rings out like the loudest crack of thunder I'd ever experienced. Billy's mouth springs open, eyes wide with disbelief. But only briefly. He falls, the life leaving his limbs almost at once, the bullet having smacked into his forehead, right between the eyes. It has blown out the back of the skull and Billy crumples into a lifeless sack of flesh. Blood blossoms around his head and somewhere a buzzard screeches, already registering dinner is about to be served.

For a moment the entire scene freezes, but within a blink or two, everyone is moving. Some run away in fear, others move towards Billy Bean's corpse. Henderson doesn't seem to know what to do.

Except me. I turn and see Pa standing on the steps of the house, his trusty Enfield musket still smoking in his hand. Somehow, I knew it was he who had fired the lethal shot and now, seeing him so impassive, I understand how hate can change a man. This was always the reason why Pa was so cold towards me. He resents me. That Ma gave birth to a son who, against all the normal emotional responses of a father, tied him to her. Forever. He yearned for his freedom. Ma was a mistake and I an even bigger one.

Our eyes meet but only for an instant. The job done, he whirls around and disappears inside the house. I hesitate for a moment and debate whether I should follow him, confront him and have it out. Clear the air once and for all. I know he will dismiss my words with disdain. I am nothing but a child. The child he never wanted. So, I turn my back on him, that house, the life I have known for fourteen years and I feel nothing.

I give Ma's grave one final look and move away. I do not turn my head to the gathering of people around Billy's body. I keep my eyes straight ahead. Brown Bear stands. His face is impassive, almost like a mirror of Pa's. In silence, we mount up and slowly lead our horses away from that hellish scene.

CHAPTER SIXTEEN

The boundaries of the ranch had barely been reached when Brown Bear reined in his horse and sat, twisting around to gaze behind him.

"What is it?" Reuben asked, pulling up next to the Indian.

Silent as the mist, Brown Bear slipped from his horse and got down on his hands and knees. Reuben watched, all of his attention on what the Indian did next.

Pressing one ear to the ground, Brown Bear remained in that position for some time until at last, he sat up, narrow eyes turned in the direction of the ranch. "Someone is trailing us," he said simply and gestured for the young man to join him.

Reuben gets down onto his knees and puts an ear close to the earth and listens, eyes closed. He strains to hear. At first, there is nothing.

"Focus all of your senses on that one spot," said Brown Bear. "Block out everything else, even my voice from now on. Let your mind penetrate deep beneath the ground. Nowhere else."

Hesitating for the briefest of moments, Reuben followed Brown Bear's instructions. Closing his eyes, he imagined himself disappearing into the earth. Blackness overcame him. The smell of damp soil, the rustle of something. An animal? Something. Concentrating with every fibre of his being, he thinks, believes ... And then, as if by magic it is there, the rumble of horses!

"My God." Unconsciously Reuben pulls out Lance's Dragoon and, after checking its load, he slips it back into his waistband. "I can hear it." Brown Bear grins. "Do we wait for whoever it is to catch up with us?"

Shrugging, Brown Bear hauled himself up onto the back of his horse. "He will not attempt anything in daylight. When we make camp, we shall be ready."

"How do you know there is only one of them?"

Brown Bear pointed to the ground. "Check for yourself again, young friend. Concentrate on your hearing and nothing more. Go ever deeper. Listen to the rhythm of the horse. Close your eyes and see it in your mind."

Without any hesitation, Reuben got down and repeated the actions, closing his eyes, his mouth set in a thin line.

"Dear Lordy," he said softly, "I can hear it!" He looked up, the wide grin splitting his face almost in two. "Lord, take my breath away but I can hear it! Brown Bear, *I can hear it*! Just like you said – there's only one."

The Indian returned the grin. "So, you can now answer your own question."

"But ..." Reuben shook his head as he put his ear to the ground for a second time. "It's so hard to tell. I wouldn't have known this sound was a rider if you hadn't told me and to guess on how many ..."

"That will come, my friend. Practise. That is the answer to mastering any skill."

"I guess that's so." Turning his face towards the way they had come, he shook his head. "Still doesn't tell us who it is, or why they're following us."

"We should ask him."

"How we gonna do that?"

Brown Bear smiled. "Wait and see."

. . .

It was in the old cabin that they readied themselves. With the horses out of sight in the surrounding woods, they settled down amongst the rocks and waited. Reuben couldn't help but glance towards where the corpses remained. Slowly decomposing, all variety of animals had chewed away at the soft body parts. As most of the dead lay amongst the trees, it had proven difficult for the buzzards to access them, but on everything else, they had feasted well.

"What a way to end your life," mused Reuben Cole out loud.

Brown Bear scoffed, "They chose their path, my friend. Do not scold yourself for what was necessary."

Reuben grunted. "I suppose."

He was about to add something more, about how he had never chosen this life for himself either. That he had dreams and hopes, none of which involved shooting people dead. But then, even as he formulated several silent responses, the rider came upon them. Tall in the saddle, a scarf around his mouth to protect him from the cold, he steered his horse to the broken steps of the cabin's entrance. He paused and scanned the surroundings before he jumped down. He looped the reins around the nearest post supporting what remained of the veranda roof and made to climb the steps.

Brown Bear emerged from one side of the cabin, Reuben from the other. They both had their guns drawn.

The man smiled. "Hello, Reuben."

"Hello, Lance." Reuben eased back the hammer of his Colt Dragoon to half-cock it. "Unbuckle your gun belt then tell us what the hell you are doing here."

"You're not gonna shoot me are you, Reubs? You wouldn't do that now, would yeh, not to your old pal?"

"Don't count on it, Lance," and to underline his words, Reuben fully cocked the massive handgun in his hand.

Lance eyed the barrel and seemed to sink within himself. He glared at Brown Bear before returning his reddening face towards Reuben. He sighed. "You an injun lover now, Reubs?"

Brown Bear's Navy was pointed unerringly towards Lance's gut. "The gun," he said quietly.

"You can't order me around, your red-skinned sonofa—"

"I can," said Reuben, his voice cold, flat, without emotion There was no disguising the meaning of his words, however, and for a moment Lance swayed a little as if suddenly weak and afraid. The tension left his shoulders and he slowly unbuckled his belt and allowed it to fall to the ground with a heavy thump.

Brown Bear moved forward and picked up the rig. Backing off, his gun still trained on the cowboy, he looped the gun belt over his shoulder.

Shaking his head, dejected, perhaps even sad, Lance breathed, "I'm disappointed in you, Reubs."

"Don't patronise me, Lance."

His head came up. "Patronise? What in the hell is that, some dumb-ass fancy way of telling me I'm an idiot? Is that it? You've had your head in your damn books for too long, boy. Instead of knowing what your station in life is, you have chosen to turn your back on your family, your *duty* and run with this ..." He jabbed a finger towards Brown Bear. "I pray that God forgives you, Reuben, because your pa sure ain't. Nor me."

"What are you talking about, Lance?"

"I'm talking about *you*. That outburst back at the ranch. You really stuck a knife into his heart with all that talk of your ma and Billy. You almost broke him."

"Broke him? That man is broken only because of his own choices! He never loved my mother, never gave her a moment of affection. Nor me, for that matter. He resented me for coming into this world and denying him his freedom to do what he wanted to do. He is selfish, cold, and heartless."

"If you didn't have that gun in your hand, or your red-skinned amigo here, I'd whup you good for what you've just said."

"Well, hell, Lance, don't let Brown Bear stop yeh. As for this," he weighed the Dragoon in his hand, eased back the hammer, and gently laid it down on a nearby rock.

"Reuben," said Brown Bear quietly, "don't do this. He will beat you."

Lance laughed at that. A great, uproarious chortle accompanied by him throwing back his head. "Hot Diggity, this is something I've been wanting to do since forever, you spoiled brat." He shot a glance towards the Indian. "You keep that itchy trigger finger under control now, boy."

"Don't interfere, Brown Bear."

Lance's grin broadened still further. "How old you now, Reubs?"

"Fifteen." He shrugged. "Almost."

"Well, that's as near to being a man as anything could be. You can take this beating like a man. It'll help you in growing up." He turned his face away and spat into the dirt. "Let's get to it."

Brown Bear stood a little way off and watched as Lance systematically and ruthlessly took Reuben apart. The young man put up a brave defence, but Lance proved too strong, too experienced. His leather-gloved fists erupted into ribs, swung into eyes and nose. A few feeble parries enabled Reuben to counter and put in the occasional dig, but Lance laughed these off. A final, heavy left hand cracked into the side of Reuben's head, dumping him unceremoniously to the ground.

Stepping back, breathing hard, but with a face full of elation, Lance grinned down at his fallen adversary. "You better stand up, boy, or I'll kick you to death right there."

"He's had enough," said Brown Bear, taking a step towards the cowboy.

"No, you stay out of this, you heathen! This boy needs to be taught a lesson."

"He's been taught."

"Not yet he ain't!"

Brown Bear watched Reuben roll over onto his knees, the blood dripping from mouth and nose. Face etched with pain, the young man looked into his friend's eyes and there was something like regret or even an admission of having made a mistake.

"Stop now, Reuben," said Brown Bear, knowing, even as he begged his young friend, that no words were ever going to dissuade him. So, he looked on as Reuben climbed unsteadily to his feet, sucked in a huge breath, crouched, turned, and swung his fist.

Lance ducked under the blow with ease, and slammed a right into Reuben's guts, folding him. A vicious left cross ended it.

Reuben lay with his nose in the dirt, the blood leaking around him. He did not move.

Brown Bear should have known what Lance would do next, but he was too stunned by Reuben's utter defeat to register anything. As he stared openmouthed, the cowboy pivoted low, his fist crunching into Brown Bear's midriff.

The air erupted out of the Indian's body and, bent double, gasping for breath, he staggered away, unable to do anything about the kick that cracked under his chin and launched him backwards. He landed flat on his back with a jolt and lay there, waves of confusion and pain flowing through him.

Seconds passed. Vaguely aware of his surroundings, he saw through a sort of mist, Lance making a grab for his gun that had fallen from Brown Bear's shoulder.

"Get up," snarled Lance, pulling back the hammer of the Navy Colt with a good deal of satisfaction. His glinting grin lent a strangely frightening wild look to his face. He seemed to be enjoying himself, this sudden turning of the tables.

Knowing there was nothing he could do but comply, Brown Bear stood up. Reuben's gun lay several feet away, too far away for him to make a move towards it. He doubted he could get his legs to work well anyway. Lance could punch, and punch hard.

"Pick up the boy and carry him into the cabin. You can then tend to him."

"I don't think I can. You must give me a moment." He shook his head. "I do not think I have ever been hit so hard."

Lance grinned. "Should have thought about that before you tried to hold me up."

"No, we did not. You followed us."

"I only wanted to know where you were going. Never thought you'd come here." He turned his head towards the cabin. "This is a dreadful place, Redskin. What happened here is something you should all leave well alone. You should never have come to this spot." He appeared to count the corpses lying close by. "What the hell are these bodies doing here?"

"These men you see, they came to kill Reuben, for what he did. We think some got away. They will be back."

"Will they, by Heaven? Well, we better move quick. I want that boy fixed up so we can go back to the ranch. Mr Cole is real sore and wants to punish his boy and hang you. As he should have done before." He chuckled. "If his boy hadn't tried to interfere, we could have all gone on living our lives."

"Is that what you think?"

"It's what I *know*, Redskin. You're vermin and like all such vermin, the only good place for you is deep in the ground. Dead."

He gestured emphatically with the gun, and Brown Bear, strength returning to his limbs, at last, went to Reuben's prone body and lifted him in his arms.

CHAPTER SEVENTEEN

I sit in a chair, pillows behind my back, damp cloth against my swollen lips. Through one half-closed eye, I view Brown Bear rinsing through another cloth, the water running red with my blood. I am amazed the water still flows so clearly from the hand pump he works at. I suspect this cabin has not been abandoned as long as it first seemed.

Across from me is Lance. He has my gun on his lap, Brown Bear's in his waistband, and his own in his now reclaimed gun belt. He looks like a one-man arsenal of death. He has more depth than I ever imagined. When I stood up to fight him, I never had an inkling just how formidable he was. He tore me apart and I didn't stand a chance. My hatred for him has gone way beyond the boundaries of nature, but that doesn't mean I do not admire him. He is not the sort of man to make an enemy of and that is precisely what I have done.

I turn my mind to what might happen next. I know Lance is not the sort of man to bargain with, that once his mind is set on a course of action, nothing will distract him from it. And yet, I am aware that those others, those men who came to kill me, will return. We could do with Lance. His skills, his expertise. In short, we need him.

"What you thinking about, boy?" he asks.

"We're in a mess, Lance." I almost laugh. This comes out as 'we're in a meth, Jeth' due to the swelling around my mouth. It was not meant to be funny and Lance, thankfully, does not react as if it were. He merely shrugs.

"So what?"

"They'll be here soon. We should get ready."

"He's right," says Brown Bear, wringing out his cloth. He has his back to me so I cannot see his face, but I can almost hear the workings of his mind.

"Then we should leave," says Lance and makes to stand.

"How do you know about this place?"

It is Brown Bear. He does not turn so I cannot read anything into his expression, but his words carry so much weight, so much intent.

"What?"

"You said it was a dreadful place, that we should not try to find out what happened. What did happen?"

I see Lance glance across to the woman, her rigid, blackened body, skin like scorched, blackened parchment, a grotesque caricature of a human being. If touched, she would disintegrate into a thousand shards of crisp, dry flesh.

"Henderson."

I almost gag. "Henderson?"

"Haven't you noticed?" Lance stoops down and picks up a discarded cigar stub. I search the floor and see there are several. "He came here to meet her. They were lovers."

"Henderson?" I said again. I couldn't believe it. I shook my head, wincing as bolts of pain race through my skull. "Henderson set this woman up here, in this remote place, to ...? No, I can't believe it."

"I don't care what you believe, boy. Henderson visited her, kept her, then when she threatened to reveal it all, he killed her."

"Why?" It was Brown Bear. "Why would he murder her for what she was to reveal? Why was it so important?"

"Never you mind, Redskin. You just get this boy patched up some more and then we'll be on our way."

"It is late. Soon it will be dark."

"You wanna stay here, with *that*?" He points to the open bedroom door and beyond it, the corpse. He crosses to the opening and stares inside. "Damn your eyes, why did you come here? Why couldn't you have left it all well alone?"

He slams the door shut and turns, looking as if he is in a frenzy, his body going into wild little spasms, head shaking, teeth gnashing. The close proximity of the woman has brought these curious changes to him, or perhaps it was the revelation about Henderson? His reaction is disturbing beyond words.

And then everything happens at once, too fast for me to register or put into any logical order.

I see Lance cocking the Dragoon and wonder, with fear, what he is to do.

In a blur, Brown Bear turns. He has his heavy-bladed hunting knife in his fist.

A horse whinnies outside. Voices chatter excitedly. It is difficult to calculate how many. More than three perhaps?

The blade thuds into Lance's chest and he gasps in surprise. Wide-eyed, he looks up and struggles to form words. But his mouth refuses to work. He crumples, the Dragoon slipping from his fingers.

Brown Bear moves like a cat and swoops up the huge revolver.

And then someone bursts through the front door.

CHAPTER EIGHTEEN

For a frozen moment, all is still. Heartbeat throbs in my throat. Beyond my control, it is my only movement as I stare at the bulk of the man filling the doorway, his face deep in shadow. A pistol erupts in flame, the explosive sound in that small space thunderous. My ears ring with it and I fall to my knees, clamping my hands across my ears.

With my head spinning with confusion and fear, I find myself drifting away into another existence, images of my mother flashing before me. She has my hand in hers and is leading me across a rolling vista of sand dunes, where small clumps of Bahia grass break through the yellow-ochre ground. The warmth of the sun on my back and the closeness of my mother combine to fill me with a delicious sense of wellbeing. All is well. I am safe.

"Lance?"

The sound of the voice snaps me back to the present. I blink several times and watch the big man stride across the room to where Lance sits pressed against the wall, his eyes wide in astonishment. His lips tremble, the voice fragile. "Oh God, Floyd, they've done for me that is for sure."

It is then, as the clouds part, that I see who the man is. Henderson drops to his haunches and bellows, "Miles, fetch water!"

As I look on in silence, I am chilled to the bone, an awful, creeping feeling which tells me that none of this going to end well.

Henderson supports Lance's head and when Miles Monroe, one of the youngest of the ranch cowboys, bursts into the room, he whips the canteen from the young man's hand and tips water into Lance's mouth.

"Easy," says Henderson as Lance coughs and splutters. I have heard it say that water is not good for a stomach wound, but in the chest, I am not so sure. Perhaps if the blade has missed the heart and the lungs, Lance might still pull through.

A movement to my left catches my attention. It is Brown Bear, clutching at one hand, blood seeping between his fingers, the ruined Colt's Dragoon lying at his feet, blown apart by Henderson's perfect shot. I go to move towards him.

"Stay put, boy!"

I snap my head towards Henderson, whose gun is trained towards me.

"Miles, you keep your pistol on that red-skinned devil. You," he waggles his gun at me, "get up and help Lance here outside."

"But Henderson, I can't—"

"Do it, or I'll put a hole in you and tell your pa it was this savage who did it. Now *move*."

There is nothing I can do, no arguments to make. My life is teetering on the edge so, despite my weakness, I go to Lance and try my best to lift him, but he is a dead-weight. Henderson gestures for Miles to help whilst he turns his gun on Brown Bear.

We stagger outside, Miles and I carrying Lance between us. I have his legs, Miles the shoulders. Lance, his eyes rolling in his head, is ashen and the knife, protruding hideously from his chest, is clearly draining him of his lifeblood. We struggle to where the horses are tethered and do our best to put him across one of the beasts' back. He groans horribly and I realise, with horror, that we have accidentally knocked the knife against the wound.

"Oh God, Miles! Get him down, quick!"

Like a mad mess of frightened animals, we lay Lance on the ground.

His breathing is laboured and the sweat across his brow is oozing like water through his pores. I know he is close to death.

"We need to take that knife out," says Miles, looking as scared as I feel.

"How we supposed to do that?"

"We just grab a hold of it and jerk it out, I guess."

"Holy sap, Miles, if we do that, he'll bleed all over us."

"Then we find something to bind him up with – you know, like bandages and the like."

"We ain't got nothing like that, Miles."

"We could use sheets from one of the beds inside the cabin. We could cut it up into strips. We used to do so during the Mexican War. Worked real good."

"But those sheets, they is filthy, Miles, even if there are any."

"Go back inside and fetch some."

I hold up my hands, the memory of the woman's corpse sitting propped up in the bed enough to turn my stomach to mush. "I ain't going back in there, Miles."

"Why not?"

"Henderson," I fire back at him, quick as anything. "He'll plug me if I go back in."

He thinks about this for a moment. It's a reasonable excuse, I feel and, by the look on his face, he seems to think so too. "If you skedaddle whilst I'm in there, I'll hunt you down, Reuben, and kill you."

"I won't go anywhere, Miles, I promise. How far you reckon I'll get anyways? I'll make sure Lance doesn't peg out but be quick. That wound looks nasty."

Without another word, Miles nods his head and rushes back into the cabin.

CHAPTER NINETEEN

Henderson waits until the others struggle outside with Lance. He then slowly crosses to the door and closes it. Brown Bear standing in the middle of the room, watches him whilst his hands are raised slightly, expressionless, resigned to what will happen next. He shows no fear because he feels no fear. He accepted death long ago and once more when they were preparing to hang him back at Reuben's ranch.

Grinning, unaware of how the Indian is feeling, Henderson scans the room, studying the corners piled up with half a lifetime of dust and debris. Next to the water pump is a haphazard clutter of metal pots and pans, long forgotten by whoever used to live here. The rickety table and chairs are eaten away by woodworm. Nothing in this building is useable. "This must have been a real nice place once."

"You remember it?"

The big man frowns. "Remember it? How can I remember a place I've never been to before, you numb-brained savage? Your English is good, but your senses are all addled. Like all you people. Thick as horse shit."

Brown Bear nods towards the closed door of the adjacent room. "And in there? How do you explain that?"

"Explain *what?*"

"Why not take a look, to remind yourself."

Henderson tilts his head, "You playing with me, boy? I could kill you right now, save Mr Cole the trouble of stringing you up."

"Either way I'll be dead."

"You're a cool one, ain't yeh?"

Henderson eased back the hammer of his pistol.

"Let me die knowing you have seen what you have done here."

"What in the hell are you talking about?"

Brown Bear nods towards the door again. "In there. You'll see."

After a short inner conversation with himself, Henderson makes up his mind and side-steps slowly towards the bedroom door, his gun always trained on Brown Bear. He eases the handle open and pushes the door inwards.

He takes a quick look.

At that precise same moment, Miles bursts into the cabin, breathless, frantic. "We need a sheet to cut up and wrap Lance's wounds. He's gonna bleed out if we don't—" He stops, snapping his head from Henderson to Brown Bear and back. "What's going on?"

The room is deathly still, nobody moving as if time itself has stopped.

Henderson lets out a long moan and stumbles into the room. Miles, after a moment's hesitation, follows him.

Brown Bear does not wait. He takes his chance and slips outside, as silent as the breeze, sees Reuben bending over Lance's prone body, and continues into the woods, disappearing amongst the trees before anyone realises he has gone.

CHAPTER TWENTY

"What is this?"

Reuben Cole returns to the cabin and slowly edges his way towards the bedroom doorway. Miles gives him a fleeting glance. Henderson stands as if struck by something, his mouth hanging open, eyes unblinking, confused, bewildered. He stares towards the bed and the corpse of the unknown woman.

"We found her when we first arrived here," Reuben explains.

"But who is she?"

"No idea. We thought maybe you might know something about it."

"*Me?*"

Henderson turns around, but he is distracted, senses still not able to understand what anything means. And as he gapes and stares, Reuben takes his chance, pulls out the gun from Miles' belt and steps back, engaging the hammer. Miles gives a strangulated squawk and Henderson groans in despair.

"Drop your gun, Floyd. I'm not taking any chances with either of you varmints."

Henderson is apoplectic with rage. He bunches his fists and roars, "*Varmints?* Who in the hell are you—"

"Just drop your gun, Floyd, or I'll drop you."

"Best do as he says," says Miles softly. He has his hands raised, his focus on the gun. "The boy is mighty mad."

"You call me 'boy' again Miles, and I'll drop you also."

In silence, Henderson drops his gun into its holster and unbuckles his belt. The rig falls to the ground with a hollow thud.

"What you gonna do now, big shot," said Henderson.

"Not what I'm gonna do, Floyd. What you are gonna do."

"I don't get you."

"Well, let me spell it out for you as you seem duller in the head than Miles here ..."

"I'm gonna whup you when this is over, boy. And I'll do it in front of your own father."

"When this is over, Floyd, you'll be dangling at the end of a rope."

Henderson's jaw dropped. "What the hell are you talkin' about, boy?"

That was enough for Reuben. Patience shattered, he sprang forward and clubbed Henderson across the nose with the barrel of the gun. The big man howled and staggered backwards, clutching at his face. He fell over the bed and landed amongst the dead girl's remains, most of her rotten bones splintering under his weight. He screamed, more from horror at being amongst the bones than from the blow to his face, rolled over and stayed there, on his hands and knees, watching the blood spot on the floor.

"I warned you," breathed Reuben. "You call me that again, I'll kill you."

"You sure has got mighty mean," said Miles.

"Well, I guess you can put a heap of blame for that on dear old Floyd's head right there."

Henderson looked up. Through a face racked in pain, his eyes burned with a fearsome intensity. He spat out a streak of blood. "I'm not gonna whup you, Reuben. I'm gonna kill yeh. First chance I get."

"I won't hold my breath. All righty, Miles. Tie up the old coot and take him outside."

"What? Are you nuts, Reuben? You surely are. Why in the hell would I wanna tie up Mr Henderson for?"

"Because he's a killer is why." And slowly, Reuben's face split with an almost maniacal grin. "He murdered that girl, right there. My only question is why."

Miles whistled softly. "And you know that for a fact?"

"I got the proof if that's what you're talking about. Now tie him up. I'm taking him down to Boniface and get the town marshal to do what he's paid to do." He cracked back the gun's hammer to full cock. "Deliver justice."

Reuben watched keenly as Miles found some strands of thin rope and bound Henderson's wrists together, tugging his hands sharply behind the big man's back. When finished, Miles stepped back.

"Who is that girl?"

"I don't know," said Reuben. "All I know is Henderson killed her, leaving her here, no doubt, because he believed no one would ever come along looking."

"That's not true," said Henderson, the sweat spouting across his brow. "I ain't ever been to this place before."

"Is that so?"

"Proof you said," put in Miles. "What proof you got, Reuben?"

"This," and Reuben brought out a cigar stub from his pocket. "They was littered across the floor here. There's only one person who smokes these, and that's you Henderson."

"You idiot. Anyone could have dropped those cigar butts. They don't mean squat and you know it."

"Do I?" He held up the cigar butt. "These here have a label. Faded they might be but clear enough to read it. Cuban. Straight out of Havana."

Squinting forward, Miles froze for a moment before he took a gulping swallow. "Dear God," he whispered. He whirled around to confront Henderson. "They is your brand, Mr Henderson! You *are* the murderer."

"You as well? You gonna be taken in by this hog's swill? This here boy has planted those cigar butts. It's all he's got."

"It's enough," said Reuben. "And why would I plant them? For what purpose? In the vain hope that you would come back here when I was waiting for you? Kind of a long shot ain't it? Nah, you killed her Henderson and then left her here to rot."

"Who is she?" Miles looked from Henderson to Reuben and back again. "*Who was she?*"

Henderson blew out his cheeks, raised his eyes to the ceiling and sighed again. "Her name was Emily Dowers. She came from New York with her husband Nathaniel to find a new life together. They built this cabin." His head came down. "But I never killed her."

Miles's eyes glared with a fiery intensity. "How come you know so much about her?"

"We became lovers."

A stunned silence settled amongst them. The others waited.

"But as I said – I didn't kill her. I swear to God."

CHAPTER TWENTY-ONE

"I t was nigh-on five or six years ago that Emily and her husband arrived in town," began Henderson. We'd put him down on a chair and Miles and me sat close around the table, me with that big old Colt pointing straight at him whilst he talked.

We listened and everything soon fell into place.

Nathaniel Dowers was a swarthy-looking individual, his chin forever covered with a smudge of beard. Keen-eyed and quick-witted, he'd worked as an accountant for a firm over in New York and when he started looking for gainful employment, the Cole ranch took him on. Old Man Cole (so-called because he was head of the family, not because he was aged. He was far from old back then) employed him to run the ranch's books and it wasn't long before he had found several discrepancies. Within three months, the ranch reported profits and Mr Cole rewarded Dowers with a raise.

It was the day Dowers brought his wife Emily to the ranch on a brand-new buggy that the problems began. Mr Cole invited the young couple to dinner, as a further reward one could say, and as she descended from the buggy, Nathaniel helping her down, Henderson saw her and almost dropped in a dead faint.

She was undoubtedly the most beautiful woman he had ever set eyes on. Her strawberry blonde hair fell loose to her shoulders, framing a face of exquisite loveliness. For a brief moment, she locked eyes with Henderson and gave him the slightest of nods. He, in turn, tipped his hat. His hand trembled and he hoped she had not noticed.

From that moment, Henderson engineered as many *accidental* meetings as he could. They exchanged formalities, a slight inclination of the head, the tiniest of smiles, but nothing more obvious than that. Inside, Henderson's body was in flames. Alone in his room at night, images of her danced across his mind, and he writhed and moaned at the thought of holding her, caressing her, loving her.

Of course, if he were honest with himself, he would have realised that none of his fantasies could ever become a reality. He was in Cole's employ as a bodyguard and was a man quick to violence, a gunhand, faster and more accurate than most. Someone to be feared. Emily's husband was intelligent, competent, a wizard with accounts. A man more valued than Henderson could ever be. What would a woman like Emily ever see in him?

When *he* first saw the reality was the day he stumbled across her in one of the ranch stables. Not the main one close to the big house, but one of the smaller ones out on the range. Mr Cole sent him there to bring in one of his mares. Mrs Cole wanted to go riding as she was feeling a little better and this particular mare, known as Belle, was the one she loved most. Henderson rode out there. It wasn't usual for him to run such an errand, but Lance was nowhere to be found.

Until Henderson found him.

He had his hand up Emily's dress and his lips pressed against hers. One long leg was wrapped around the range boss and both hands clawed at his hair. As Lance lifted her into his arms and carried her to a pile of fresh hay, Henderson watched them from the doorway, consumed with jealousy and hate.

He bided his time. He watched. He took to following her as best he could, but often this was difficult but over the next days and weeks, he catalogued every one of their liaisons. The morning she went missing, Nathaniel rode into the house, beside himself with despair. Old Man Cole summoned Henderson to find her. Which he did, dishevelled and naked on the bed at Dower's cabin. But not as she was once was. She'd been shot dead.

Henderson stumbled out of the cabin as if afflicted with some horrific sickness, unable to speak, barely able to walk. He rode out to the large cluster of buttes some miles from the ranch, and sat there, lamenting for a life he would never know and the woman he had loved.

Could it have been Lance? But why, why kill her when they were obviously consumed by the passion of each other? Henderson couldn't work it out. Upon his return to the big house, Lance was already there, nonchalant, unconcerned. His cool demeanour, however, caused Henderson to believe that, despite his ardour, Lance knew absolutely what Emily's fate had been.

"But you have no proof," said Reuben when Henderson had come to the end of his tale. "You didn't actually see Lance kill her, did you."

Henderson, his eyes wet and red-rimmed, struggled to keep his voice even. "It's obvious."

"Is it? I think what is more obvious is that your jealousy caused you to murder her."

"It sure does seem that way, Mr Henderson," put in Miles, subdued.

"I've told you the truth," said Henderson.

"So why didn't you tell anyone what you'd found?" Reuben leaned forward. "All these years, leaving her here, to rot in that bed. What sort of a man are you to do that?"

"I didn't ..." Exasperated, Henderson slapped both hands over his face despite the cords binding his wrists together. "Don't you think I've thought of doing just that?"

"So why didn't you?"

Henderson dropped his hands and glared at Miles. "Less than a fortnight later we came across Nathaniel Dowers dangling from a rope. Heartbroken, he'd hanged himself. I hold myself responsible because it was the not knowing that killed him, the poor sap. If I had told him what I knew then perhaps ... But I couldn't. I couldn't let him see her that way. I intended to return, to bury her properly but when he took his own life it all became so ... unnecessary. Time moved on and I put it out of my mind, eventually."

"And what about Lance? You never confronted him with what you knew?"

"No, never. But when you announced you'd been chased here by those varmints you'd tried to protect Brown Bear from, I knew Lance would follow you. So, I followed him."

"You mean it was Lance who planted those cigar butts," said Miles, "to put suspicion on you?"

"Is that it, Henderson?" said Reuben, his eyes never leaving his father's bodyguard. "Is that what you think has happened?"

Henderson held Reuben's stare. "I can't think of anything else. Once it had got out that Emily is lying here, shot to pieces, there'd be hell to pay. Lance knew I had feelings for her. I suspect your father did also. It would be easy to place the blame on me."

Leaning back in his chair, Reuben considered the big man sitting across the table from him for some time. His explanation made sense. Lance was clever, resourceful. If anybody could engineer such a deceitful scenario it was he. He blew out a loud sigh. "There's one thing I just don't get," he said slowly, airing his thoughts, "why would Lance kill her that way? If he loved her, I mean."

"As you also did..." said Miles Monroe, staring at the floor.

"I ... I've tried to work it out all these years. I don't honestly think Lance did kill her. I think it was her husband, consumed with jealousy. That's what I reckon."

"How did he know?"

"Perhaps she told him, who knows. I can't see Lance killing her, no matter what he's tried to do to frame me."

"And there's another little worry I have. Why would Lance frame *you*, why not just confront the husband, bring him to justice. *If*, of course, he was the killer?"

"I can't answer that. Lance has always been jealous of my relation-ship with your father, the trust we have. Perhaps he had designs on bettering himself in the ranch."

"Promotion? By framing you with Emily's murder?" Reuben waited, but with Henderson slipping into a moody silence, he nodded towards Miles. "Untie him and let's go and talk to Lance. Maybe then we can get some straight answers."

"If he's still alive."

"Yeah ... *if* he's still alive."

Stepping outside all three froze on the first step of the cabin.

Lance was not lying on the ground.

Lance had disappeared.

CHAPTER TWENTY-TWO

Old Bill Night ran the whorehouse in the town of Saint Boniface, and he was as flea-ridden as the establishment he oversaw. Most days, and evenings for that matter, he whiled away the hours on a rickety rocking chair, sipping whisky from a stone jug, watching the world go by with the same weary acceptance he felt about his past life. A long time ago, he wandered the range, a bounty hunter looking for the many and varied pickings that were so richly scattered across the West. Having accrued enough money, he bought himself a saloon in the town of Saint Boniface and settled into a steady rhythm, eventually extending his business to include a bordello. Often, he would partake of the delights offered by his employees, but many years had passed since he last felt even the slightest stirrings for such indulgences. When two years before, Nancy arrived from Chicago, as pretty as a spring morning with her ash-blonde hair piled high on her head, waist-coat pulled in tight around the waist, and her backside so plump there was not the faintest raising of heartbeat, no breaking out in a sweat. Nothing. Old Bill knew then that life was nothing but a waiting parlour for the inevitable.

Below him, sprawled across the steps, Joshua LeMar plucked away at his banjo. Joshua was as mean as a rattler with a toothache and strapped to the back of his banjo was a Wells Fargo Navy with which he often used to shoot passing strangers. Since Sheriff Morris passed away last fall, there was no law in Saint Boniface and Bill preferred it that way. It brought a degree of freedom to his business. If anyone stepped out of line, it was down to him to fix it. Or Joshua, now that Old Bill was a lot slower, his knees swollen up like knots in a tree, his hands bent with the fingers more like claws than the nimble digits they once were. He liked Joshua and kept him on side, plying him with drinks and the occasional free ride with one of the girls. Joshua repaid the kindness by watching Old Bill's back. It was a mutually beneficial arrangement and had been so for at least half a dozen years. Neither saw any reason why it should change.

Bill Night dozed, but with the sun diffuse, the white mist of winter easing its usual intensity which sucked the life out of the earth and bleached the buildings which ran down either side of the town's only street, it was difficult. In the summer months, people baked inside their homes and shops as if they were bread rolls in an oven. In the winter, they shivered, numb with cold. This was such a morning and he pondered on going indoors and warming himself in front of the fire when a man came riding into sight. Joshua saw him first, grunted and sat up. Old Bill turned his scrawny chicken-neck and frowned. It was rare for anyone to arrive in the town nowadays, even rarer was a lone rider, let alone one like this. Lean, dressed in a white shirt which accentuated the blood dried up across the front. Old Bill measured him and decided the man had either been shot or stabbed. From this distance, he could not tell. He noted the man did not bear a handgun, only an old muzzle-loading carbine in a scabbard attached to the saddle. The most disturbing aspect of the stranger, however, was the man's pallor. Blood loss would kill him for sure.

"Go check him out, Josh."

Grunting again, Joshua gave a final strum of his banjo and stood up. Checking both ends of the street, he stepped down from the saloon and ambled across towards the stranger.

Old Bill continued to watch. He turned his head and called into the saloon, "Katrina. Bring me the sawn-off." Studying the stranger again, the way his head lolled from side to side the way it did, the hand not holding the reins hanging limp and heavy, it was clear that he was in no condition to cause any kind of threat, but Old Bill was not the sort to take chances. As Katrina stepped out into the sunlight, squinting in the glare, he snatched the gun from her and quickly checked the load. "Get back inside," he snapped, and Katrina did so, pausing for a moment to tell Old Bill the saloon was low on whisky. He sneered and turned his attention once more to the stranger.

With his eyes locked on the suffering rider, reassuring himself that there was no weapon in his waistband, Joshua took out the Wells Fargo from the back of his banjo and eased himself next to the horse. Slinging the musical instrument over his shoulder, he gently took hold of the reins, stopping the horse from continuing. Noticing the sudden halt of his mount's progress, the stranger's head came up.

"Friend," said Joshua through gritted teeth, "you look in a might awful way. We ain't got no doctor here but we can get you into the saloon. Some of the girls know a thing or two about patching up wounds and the like. You been shot?"

The stranger shook his head, an action that caused him some distress. He winced, sucking in breath with a hiss. "A knife. Deep."

Joshua put the Wells Fargo into his waistband and stretched out his arms, "Let me take your weight, friend. I'll get you to the saloon. Knife wounds is just about the worst."

The stranger allowed himself to fall into Joshua's strong arms. He groaned, blood leaking from the wound to splash across Joshua's shirt front.

"Hell, we need to get you fixed real quick."

"I took it out," said the stranger.

"Jeez, not sure if that was the right thing to do, friend." He turned his head to the steps of the saloon and whistled loudly. "Old Bill, get someone to take this man's horse to the livery. Then tell the girls to clear a table. He's gonna need patching up and real quick. He's bleeding out, Old Bill."

It all happened very quickly from that point. From nowhere the stranger seemed to gather whatever remaining energy he had, reached for Joshua's Wells Fargo, and tugged it free.

"Oh my," said Joshua.

The stranger shot him through the gut and Joshua fell to the ground, rolling around and squawking, clutching at the dreadful wound to his midriff, the blood gushing between his fingers. "He's killed me, Bill. He's killed me."

The stranger shot Joshua twice more to silence him before striding across the street towards the saloon.

"Oh my God," breathed Bill and stood up, his old legs wobbling beneath him. There was little strength left in them and he could not remain standing for long. Even so, he managed to bring up the shotgun and discharge one barrel. The stranger, however, was out of range, the pellets scattering harmlessly in a wide spread. The stranger continued to come forward.

Flopping down into his rocking chair, Old Bill cursed every single entity that anyone had ever believed in and tried in vain to shoot again.

The man came up the steps, the Wells Fargo pointed straight ahead. "Drop it."

Old Bill sagged, collapsing into himself, the shotgun clattering to the floor. "You had no need to kill Josh like that, mister. He was only trying to help."

"Girls he said," the stranger continued, dismissing Old Bill's words as if he'd never heard them. "They can patch me up, he said. So, tell 'em to set to it." He eased back the hammer of the gun, "Or I'll blow your withered head off, old man."

As things turned out, Old Bill did not need to call out to anyone. Katrina was already coming through the batwing doors at a rush. In her hands was a long-handled shovel which she swung in a wide arc. Before the stranger had a chance to turn, the heavy flat of the spade slapped across the side of his head and he fell to the ground with a dull thud, unconscious.

"You get the girls to tie this varmint up," wheezed Old Bill, a trembling hand wiping away the sweat rolling down his face, "and then we'll hang him right out here in the street."

"You betcha," said Katrina as she leaned on the spade to admire her handiwork.

CHAPTER TWENTY-THREE

"This is proof he did it, all right," said Miles Monroe, as the three of them set off on their mounts in pursuit of Lance.

"It sure seems that way," grunted Henderson, lighting up a cigar. Clamping it into the corner of his cruel mouth, he shot a hateful glare towards Reuben. "I'd say you owe me an apology, boy."

"I told you, and I won't tell you again, you call me *boy* one more time and I'll put you in the ground."

"Now hold on there," said Monroe quickly, "there ain't no need to continue this feud any longer. We have to work together to catch Lance and take him back to the ranch so Mr Cole can question him and somehow get to the truth of all this."

They edged their horses into the surrounding wood, each man mindful of overhanging boughs, dipping their heads every few paces.

"I think that's probably for the best," added Monroe, "if that poor girl is ever gonna get some kind of justice.

"And I want that apology," growled Henderson.

"If Lance tells it the same way, you'll get it Henderson," said Reuben, scouring the ground for any signs. His mind was more on Brown Bear at that moment and where his friend may have got to. Men like Henderson acted first, then asked questions. He would have shot Brown Bear dead before he'd even scratched the surface of the truth. The Indian had done the right thing in getting away but where he was and what he was going to do were mysteries to Reuben. He couldn't explain it, but he just knew Brown Bear was somewhere close, watchful, biding his time but for what, Reuben could not begin to fathom.

It was as they emerged from the far side of the wood that they first spotted the riders. Reuben counted four. They did not appear to be in any particular hurry, but they were heading in the general direction of the cabin.

Reuben knew instinctively who they were. "We better dismount and take cover," he said.

"You think those are the same ones who tried to shoot you up, Reuben?"

Reuben nodded towards Monroe, "It's hard to tell but why else would four men be coming this way?"

"Well, we ain't got much choice but to hole up here," said Henderson, gripping his saddle pommel. "Lance took the horse with the only carbine we got so we'll have to engage 'em close up."

"*Engage?*" squawked Monroe. "What in the hell does that mean?"

"It means," said Henderson, lowering himself to the ground, "that them is killers and they won't be in any mood to talk about the weather."

"But shoot, Mr Henderson, I ain't no gunfighter. I'm a cowboy and I never—"

"Well, now's the time to learn, Monroe. Check your load and then take the horses out of sight. Make sure you hobble 'em because when the shooting starts, they'll be spooked."

"I don't think I can go through with—"

"Just do it. *Now.*"

For a moment it seemed Monroe might argue his point still further but when Henderson placed hands on hips and gave him a hard stare, the young cowboy turned away, defeated. Reuben watched him trudge away with the horses.

"What about you, Reuben? Are you up to this?"

Reuben turned to hold Henderson's stare. "Whatever it takes."

"You've grown up awful fast these past few days, ain't yeh?"

"I ain't yet seen fifteen, as well you know, but none of that matters anymore. I've killed men and if I don't do it again this time …" He looked towards the riders, "Well, they will certainly kill me."

"I misjudged you."

"Why? Because I'm a killer now?"

"No. Because you understand that life rarely deals you a good hand. It's how you play the game that counts. Not just the killin'."

"I wish I'd never done it. Wish I'd never gone out on that ride. Wish I'd never laid eyes on Brown Bear."

"That's a whole lot of wishes. You can't undo what's done, Reuben. What you need to do now is live with it, or at least find a way to do so."

"What I need to do right now," he said with a sigh as he drew his handgun, "is try and get out of this situation alive."

Turning his head towards the approaching riders, Henderson pulled in a large breath. "We get under cover and we don't open up until they is almost on top of us. Don't shoot until I do, you understand?"

Reuben nodded. "I do. I've only got six shots though."

"Then you make every one of them tell. Aim big and when a man falls, you shoot him again."

With no time to ask any more questions, Reuben broke off, running towards the undergrowth clumping between the trees. He had no sense of where Henderson had gone as his concentration now centred on finding his own place to hide. Even so, as he plunged deeper into the eerie darkness of the forest, a shooting glance to his left brought him to a grinding stop.

Monroe stood rooted, like the trees, unmoving, staring at something. Reuben wanted to call out but had neither the strength nor the sense to do so. Fear gripped him. The riders were closing, and he could hear their voices, smell the stench of horse sweat. And yet Monroe stood with his back towards the men as if in some sort of trance.

And then, without any seeming reason for such a thing, he fell face-first into the ground. Reuben watched but he could not understand. Death, as silent as the night, had enveloped him.

Enveloped them all.

CHAPTER TWENTY-FOUR

O ld Bill's first swinging fist smashed under Lance's ribs with the power of a mule's kick, causing the wound in his chest to erupt and spew out a stream of blood. Lance screamed. This didn't stop Old Bill, it spurred him on. "You killed my best friend," he snarled and landed a hefty left across Lance's jaw, snapping the cowboy's head right back. Norton, the bartender, and Sarah, a huge, great lumbering whore with arms like tree trunks, held up the hapless Lance. From all around the saloon interior, a half dozen girls cackled with glee. Everyone was having a good time.

Apart from Lance, of course, who was gulping down blood and snot as it bubbled and frothed in his throat.

"Careful you don't kill him before we string him up," said Norton.

It was timely advice. Not through any sense of mercy, but simply because he was close to exhaustion, Old Bill relented and stumbled backwards to fall into a chair, wheezing loudly. "Give me a beer."

"Fetch Old Bill a drink one of yeh!"

Katrina swiftly dipped behind the bar and placed a dusty glass beneath the hand-drawn beer pump. The pale-coloured beer surged over the rim, the creamy froth making up more than half the volume, but she brought it to Old Bill nevertheless, who drank it down with great gusto.

He dragged one gnarled hand across his mouth, smacking his lips. "That tasted good. Fetch me another."

Katrina did so. With this one, Old Bill took his time.

"Drag him outside," he said after a moment. "We'll string him up in front of Carl Malone's merchandise store. His sign has a good strong metal supporting post."

"Malone's gone and left town early this morning, Old Bill," said Sarah, sweating with the exertion of keeping Lance on his feet.

"You're thinking I need to ask his permission?"

She shrugged. "Could be. But from what I gather, he ain't coming back. Says this town is dead and he's gone to seek his fortune elsewhere. So yeah, you do what you think is right."

"Shoot, Sarah, you has the mind of a child."

"And the body of a male bison," added Norton, running his tongue along his lower lip.

"Anything male is what makes you manage it, Nort," returned Sarah, throwing her head back in a loud guffaw. The other girls squealed.

"Never heard you complain," said Norton, somewhat hurt.

"That's 'cause I couldn't speak due to me laughing so much!"

"Is he a tiddly," shouted another young whore from the corner.

"Like a tadpole."

The room's ceiling almost collapsed with the uncontained laughter of those watching.

Red-faced, Norton swung away, releasing his hold on the cowboy. "I'll not listen to this."

Sarah also released her grip and Lance fell with a crash to the floor. Sarah, blowing out a sigh of gratitude for the loss of her burden, leaned across the counter to Katrina who still stood there. "How's about a beer for me, my little one?"

Katrina gave her colleague a long look. Nevertheless, she poured her out a glass of beer.

"Let's get him outside," said Old Bill in a tired voice. "I'm sick of looking at his face."

. . .

Crouching outside beside the saloon's batwing doors, lost in the shadows cast by the veranda roof, Brown Bear heard every word. Escaping in fear of his life, he'd disappeared into the woods and planned to return to help Reuben escape when the time was right. Those plans, however, changed dramatically when Lance staggered to his feet and hauled himself painfully across Reuben's horse. Brown Bear watched him in stunned silence as the wounded cowboy slipped away. Rousing himself, he'd tracked Lance with ease, following him all the way into the town, believing he could, in some way, convince Lance to return to the Reuben ranch, give his version of events, face up to the consequences, and so return Reuben to his father's good books.

But then he'd witnessed the killing of the banjo-player and he realized, once more, that plans would need to change.

So here he squatted, waiting.

CHAPTER TWENTY-FIVE

Gunfire erupted without warning. Reuben sprang to his feet almost before Henderson's words screamed out, "Open-up on 'em, open-up on 'em!"

He stepped into another world. In a blinding instant of fear and confusion, the surrounding forest, so recently tranquil and serene, was now a killing ground. Men desperately battling to keep terrified horses under control, fired without aiming while Henderson, standing so tall, so large, loosed off his rounds with great precision.

Running, bent-double, Reuben made for the nearest piece of cover – a fallen tree trunk, old and gnarled but thicker than a steer. Diving across it, he rolled over, chanced a look, and watched, mesmerised, as Henderson shot a man from the saddle, sending him spinning to the earth, blood spewing from his chest. Another bullet rang out to hit the fallen man in the head before the others gathered their senses and returned fire in a much more controlled way.

Three men, all on horseback, their mounts screaming, turning, kicking, and fighting. Another fell, the bullet blowing out the top of his shoulder. He screamed and the two remaining riders decided their best bet was to dismount.

They did so, but not in an orderly way. Flinging themselves to the ground, their horses, relieved to be free, sped off in a mad gallop. Rolling under whatever cover they could find, the two men loosed off shot after shot.

At some point, Henderson buckled and pitched to his side. He managed to remain on one knee, but as Reuben studied him, he saw the blood trailing down his smashed wrist. His gun hand was ruined.

Seemingly unconcerned, Henderson reached into the depths of his thick overcoat to produce another gun. From his kneeling position, he squeezed off two more shots before a bullet hit him in the throat.

Reuben's mouth fell open and watched as if in a dream, an eerie greyness descending over the scene. Henderson keeled like a great tree, the strength gone from his body. No more control. No more life. He smacked into the forest floor and remained still.

Dead.

Crying out, Reuben broke cover. With no time to think, convulsed by an irresistible force, he strode across the open ground, his handgun thrust forward, all his concentration fixed upon the two remaining men. They gaped, wide-eyed, disbelieving, and fired off a wild fusillade.

Reuben continued to march. At ten paces or so, he stopped, held his breath, and shot the first man between the eyes. The other stood, threw out his arms, and shook his head violently.

Reuben shot him in the chest, throwing him back against the closest tree, sliding down into a sitting position. He stared, mouth trying to form words and Reuben shot him again, this time in the head.

For the briefest of moments, silence descended. Not a natural, welcome silence, but one which seemed to contain nothing but foreboding. Reuben could never explain it, but something, a message or warning from out of the air, ethereal, inexplicable caused him to turn. In a half-crouch, he twisted, the gun close to his hip, the left palm fanning the hammer.

Three bullets hit the approaching stranger, the man whom Reuben later discovered had killed Monroe. He crumpled, the bow he carried, that silent tool of death, falling beside him.

. . .

The stillness penetrated deep into his very bones as Reuben flopped down on a fallen tree and methodically reloaded his pistol with cap and ball he'd taken from one of the dead men. He shivered and turned eyes skyward. The thin covering of white clouds gave everything an unearthly feel as if somehow, he had slipped into another existence far from this world. All-consuming and depressing, the heaviness of the atmosphere settled around him and would not let him go.

After some moments, he went to Henderson's body, reached into the big man's pocket, and found a cigar, together with a small silver box which contained some matches. He studied the cigar for several minutes, rolling it in his fingers, then stuck it into his mouth, lit it and drew in the tobacco.

Instantly seized by an uncontrollable fit of violent coughing, he doubled-up and retched, felt the bile coming up into his throat and threw away the smoke in disgust.

He stood up shakily, pressing the back of his hand into each watering eye, and having regained some of his composure, he did his best to check the other bodies, kicking them in the side to see if they stirred.

One, a thin, wiry individual, moaned as Reuben's boot connected with his ribs. Without a pause, Reuben knelt, deftly relieved the man of his gun, and tossed it out of reach.

"Mercy," the man managed to say, the blood dribbling from his mouth as he spoke. His teeth, the few that remained, were also awash with blood. Reuben knew without checking for the wound, that the man was shot clean through the gut. He would be dead within the hour. "For the love God, I'm begging you ..."

Reuben put an index finger across the man's mouth. "It's all right, try not to agitate yourself too much."

With surprising speed and strength, the man's hand streaked forward, seizing Reuben's forearm. "I'm gonna die, ain't I? Oh, sweet Jesus, don't let me die!"

"You need to hush," Reuben said, doing his best to sound reassuring. He tried in vain to remove the man's grip of steel. "I'll fetch you some water."

"No, please, don't leave me alone."

"I'll be but a moment," said Reuben, again doing his utmost to break himself free. The man held on, however, if anything more strongly than before. A feverish, wild expression in his eyes brought home to Reuben how terrified the dying man was.

"The Injun. It is all the fault of what we did. He killed me."

Reuben blinked back his surprise. "What? No, no, he's gone. He ..." He stopped, not wishing to expand on the truth. He knew also it was futile. The man was beyond comprehending anything.

"We should never ... We should never have listened to Banner. None of it had nothing to do with any of us. If only I had stayed at the fort. If only ..." Gripping Reuben's arm stronger than before, the man levered himself into a sitting position. Through his quivering lips, his voice rattled, "I see him. I see him coming."

"Who? Who do you see coming?"

The man's head snapped around, his wild gaze burning into Reuben's. "He's here and he's come to kill me. I'm sorry. Sweet Jesus, I'm sorry."

The bullet hit the man between the eyes, hurling his broken body back into the dirt. Reuben swung around, bringing his own gun to bear.

For the briefest of moments, he stared into the face of the man who had engineered it all. The one called Banner. Reuben flung himself to his right as the man's handgun erupted into flame. Rolling over and over, he knew he must keep himself a moving target or else it would be over. With little opportunity to bring his own gun to bear, he continued to roll until he reached a clump of sage and scurried deep within the brittle yet sharp branches.

The pain screamed through his shoulder. He hadn't noticed it until he came to a halt. He now realised he'd been shot. With little time to react, he pushed the agony away and chanced a look. He saw the hulking Banner frantically reloading. Reuben brought up his gun and fired. One, two, three bullets. All of them went wide, but they had the desired effect and Banner turned and bolted, thrashing into the depths of the trees, swallowed up by the murkiness. Gone.

Reuben remained amongst the scrub, not daring to emerge until he was certain Banner had left. Reassured, he stood and immediately sucked in a sharp breath through his teeth, the pain in his shoulder burning with an intensity, unlike anything he had ever experienced. Shoving his gun into his waistband, he gingerly probed the wound with his fingers and sighed with relief. The bullet had grazed the flesh, creating a deep furrow across his shirt. The blood oozed and it hurt like sin but at least the bullet was not inside. Ripping away his neckerchief, he fashioned it into a ball and padded the wound with it to stem the bleeding. Then he busied himself reloading his pistol. There were plenty of other firearms scattered around, together with various items he could use. His first problem, however, was to find a horse. They had all bolted. Monroe had not been able to hobble their mounts before he was killed, so they too had gone. Without a horse, he wasn't going to get very far in this cold.

Taking a final look around and assuring himself Banner had gone, he slowly and methodically moved through the trees until, at last, he found a pair of horses quietly grazing at some tufts of coarse grass. He almost swooned with relief.

CHAPTER TWENTY-SIX

Mitch was tired. He'd slept in the saddle but now, stretching out his back, every muscle and tendon ached in a way that made him think his body had turned to stone. Pulling up his horse, he looked across the endless plain stretching out towards the far horizon. Seeing the distant mountains, misty grey in the cold morning light, he realised he still had a considerable way to go before he reached Fort Defiance, the place he believed young Reuben had headed for. But that was before he'd heard the gunfire. He'd therefore skirted further west, not willing to become embroiled in any firefight, no matter who was doing the shooting. He knew Arapaho continued to roam this area and rumours had circulated for some time that raiding parties, close to starvation, had attacked homesteads. People had died. Mitch was one man and although he was good with a gun, he doubted he could last long against a marauding group of desperate Indians.

Riding around the forest which separated the prairie into two distinct parts, he came to a rise and there, far below, a town. It had to be Saint Boniface. With no idea what awaited him there, he moved on at a more cautious pace.

He'd spotted the Indian a little later. Squinting across the rolling landscape, Mitch noted that the man was on foot and was moving with an even, loping gait. Furthermore, it was clear he was heading towards the town. Now why would that be, mused Mitch, rubbing his chin. Did that mean Reuben was in the town? Alone? The of them, Reuben and the savage had left the ranch together so had they become separated? When Mr Cole summoned them together in the library, he'd stood with his head bowed, holding his hat in front of his groin, moving it around in a circle. Ahead of him was Mr Henderson and Lance. Both of them seemed agitated by something. Mitch could guess what it was but kept it all to himself.

"I want you to bring him back," Mr Cole was saying, sat behind his great desk, his eyes wet with tears. "I shouldn't have said the things I said. He's my only son and I don't want him killed by those ... those murdering scum from out of Fort Defiance. You hear me, Henderson?"

"I do indeed, Mr Cole," Henderson had said, straight-backed, proud as ever. "I'll bring him back."

"A cabin he said," put in Mr Cole. "Something about a cabin. You think he'll head there?"

"It could be the place to start."

"Or maybe he'll make for Defiance," Mitch had said, not knowing it was his place to say so, but putting in the suggestion even so.

Mr Cole stared directly at him, and Mitch prepared himself for an admonishment. It never came. Instead, Mr Cole let out a long, low sigh. "Yes. That's where you found out about this varmint Banner wasn't it, Lance?"

"It was, Mr Cole, but I don't think—"

Cole waved any objections away. "You head for the fort, Lance. Henderson, you go directly to the cabin. Take Monroe."

Mr Cole stood and turned to the window. The conversation was over. Mitch stepped aside to allow the senior ranch hands to leave the room. Settling his hat on his head, Mitch made as if to follow them.

"Mitch," said Cole, his voice like the crack of a whip. "You stay here. I want to talk to you." Mitch frowned, perplexed, and looked at his boss. "Close that door, I don't want no one listening in to what I have to say to you."

Obediently, Mitch pressed the great, heavy library door closed and turned.

"Sit down, Mitch. I need to talk to you man-to-man."

Confused, Mitch pulled out a chair and slowly sat opposite his employer, the man he'd served for over six years. A man he respected. A man he had never seen looking so lost, so in despair.

"I know there ain't no love lost between Henderson and Lance," he began, sitting back in his swivel chair, staring at the ceiling. "That's why I didn't want them both going to the cabin. You know the reasons why, don't you, Mitch?" He returned to his seat, moving his head slightly to study Mitch with keen interest.

Mitch had his hat in his lap now, running the brim through his fingers, like before. He was nervous, bemused. He didn't know where any of this was heading. "A little, Mr Cole."

"I think you know more than a little, Mitch. You and she, you were lovers weren't you."

Mitch brought his head up and gazed with alarm at his boss. "Mr Cole, I don't know what you—"

"Save it," snapped Cole. "You think I'm some sort of dunderhead like all the others do? You think since I stopped riding out to oversee the ranch for myself, I've become dim-witted and ignorant, sitting here at my desk with nothing to do but sip whisky? And now with Mrs Cole gone, you think I have sunk even deeper within myself."

"That's not true, Mr Cole. Everyone respects and admires you."

"Respect and admiration have got nothing to do with it. I may not be out there, roping steers, breaking horses, but I know what goes on, Mitch. I know about you and Lance and that damn woman."

"Mr Reuben—" Aghast, Mitch half raised himself from his chair, "I'm not sure you have it right. What happened between me and ... well, it wasn't the same as the untidy mess she had with Lance. It's not fair for you to—"

"I never said it was fair, Mitch. Any of it. Relax, I know everything about what went on with you all and that damned woman. You loved her, am I right?"

Mitch stared, unable to vocalise any of the numerous thoughts racing around his head. "I, er, I don't rightly know, Mr Cole."

"You had feelings for her, as did Henderson and Lance."

"*Lance*? Lance had no feelings for her, Mr Cole. He was only out to get what he could from her. There was no ... Mr Henderson, I know he felt a good deal for her, romantically like. But he is a gentleman, a man of honour. He never once forced himself upon her, unlike Lance. Lance was ... Hell, Mr Cole, do you want me to spell it out?"

"I'd appreciate it, Mitch."

Mitch ballooned his cheeks. "It ain't a pretty story, Mr Cole."

"I think I've already guessed that. Tell it, Mitch."

"All right. Lance visited her regularly and the more he visited the more he became obsessed. Mr Henderson, he found out. Nigh-on broke his heart, I reckon."

"And you?"

"Hell, I didn't have all that much to do with her, if I'm honest, despite my feelings for her."

"If you're honest?" Cole's grin seemed more like a sneer from where Mitch was sitting. "Don't insult my intelligence, Mitch."

Breathing hard, Mitch pulled off his neckerchief and dabbed at his brow. "Well, seeing as you obviously know ... Yeah, it's true. I had relations with her. Lots of times."

"When Lance was out on the range."

"If Lance had found out, he'd have shot me stone dead."

"I'm thinking maybe he did find out, Mitch."

"Not as far as I know."

"She was a married woman, Mitch. Did that never enter into your dealings with her? Both you and Lance ... Dear Lord, what he did to that poor man. Her husband. Drove him to his death is what happened."

"That's as may be, Mr Cole, but that wasn't down to me. He'd come across Lance and her. It was because of Lance that he—"

"You are as much to blame as Lance, you simpleton." Cole swung in his chair to face Mitch directly. He moved forward, resting his elbows on the desk. "Henderson knew about her and Lance, but I think he may have been ignorant of your involvement. Which is why you're still alive."

"You ain't gonna tell him, are you, Mr Cole?"

"Do I look like an idiot?" He held up a hand quickly. "Don't answer that. No, Mitch, I need you alive. Good men are hard to find these days, especially ones who can shoot. And the way things are going in Washington ... Well, I need continuity and normality, as far as that is possible. I want you to shadow them and make sure they don't end up killing each other. You return my boy, safe and sound, and then we go back to business. Like it was before all this nonsense took hold of our lives. You give them a good head start and then you follow them. I know you're good, Mitch. Reward the faith I have in you."

"Yes sir, Mr Cole, I will."

"Good, now get yourself a good horse and a couple of days provisions and bring my boy home."

Now, watching the Indian moving easily towards the town, Mitch had an awful feeling of foreboding. Where was Reuben, and did all that gunfire he'd heard have anything to do with it? Had he got himself into a gunfight? He was barely fifteen and, as far as Mitch knew, didn't have much inkling about going up against gunmen intent on killing him. He was brave, no denying that. The way he'd stood up against Lance so many times proved it, but gunfighting, that was different.

Hopefully, he'd get some answers in the town. Rolling his shoulders, Mitch steered his horse down the slight incline towards Saint Boniface.

CHAPTER TWENTY-SEVEN

He had a rough idea in which direction to go. Tramping through the trees, Reuben came to the tracks left by the men who had come to kill him. He followed them, as best he could, across the rolling plain. The ground was hard due to the intense cold and very few hoof-prints were visible. He'd gathered what provisions he could from his fallen attackers, stripping one of the two horses he'd found of bedroll, water, hardtack, and ammunition before setting it free. He had another Halls carbine together with a brace of pistols. If he could not find his way to the town of Saint Boniface then he felt confident he could survive on the plains, exposed as he was to the harsh elements. If need be, he'd turn towards the ranch and make his way home.

Of course, if he'd thought about it, the tracks would lead him to Fort Defiance, the place he knew Banner's men had come from. Pulling on the reins, he brought his horse to a halt and stared across an endless plain, the expanse of rough, hard earth hyphenated by the occasional pieces of scrub, a panorama of despair if he were honest with himself.

The snow came, without warning. His ability to read the signs was not yet sufficiently developed so when the weather turned, he was caught unawares. Pulling his jacket close around his throat, he bent low over the neck of his horse and tried as best he could to continue forward.

With the wind howling and the cold virtually calcifying his bones, he knew he had to find shelter soon. If he were caught out here as night fell, exposed to the elements, he would freeze to death. Lost as he was, with no way of seeing any tracks, not knowing which direction to take, the sun obscured by the swirling whiteness, his only hope was that the weather might clear. He prayed for it. Constantly. Squeezing his eyes shut, he trusted in his horse to find the best way to some sort of salvation.

The heavy plod of the animal's hooves sounded like a metronome of doom. He did not know how long he and the horse walked. Bundled up in his coat, inadequate as it was, Reuben shivered so violently his teeth clattered in his mouth. His leather riding gloves gave him little protection. His ears and nose were alive with pain. He could no longer feel his toes. A yawning blackness overwhelmed him, and he held onto his horse's mane and did his best not to think wistfully of home, log fires, and his mother's gentle, reassuring voice. He was not yet fifteen and, despite having killed, he was not yet a man of strength or courage. Fear bubbled away in his guts, fear the like of which he had never known before. Chancing a look forward all he could make out was an impenetrable curtain of white. The blizzard was all-consuming, and it seemed endless. No respite given. He groaned, pressed his face deeper into his horse's neck and prayed again.

Soon he could no longer think or pray. Blackness, soothing and warm, slowly overcame him and even though he knew he should not sleep he no longer had the strength, or the will, to stop himself.

The first inkling he had of someone close was when he blinked open his eyes and stared skywards to a vista of brilliant blue. The storm had passed, and he was alive. As the realisation crept into his senses, a shadow moved across him, blocking out the sun.

"Boy, you sure is one difficult person to find."

Frowning, Reuben tried to make out the owner of the voice, but all he had was the silhouette in front of his eyes. It was only when the man stooped down that Reuben could see his face. He gasped, went to sit up, and Mitch gently pressed him back down.

"You rest up, young fella. I got us a fire going and have stacked you up with blankets and the like. Coffee will be coming shortly."

Bewildered, Reuben tried to speak, but his throat was dry, constricted, and his lips, when he went to open his mouth, cracked.

"Don't try to talk none. Once you get some hot food and coffee inside you, things will get easier. Until then, you just rest."

"Horse ..."

"What's that? Your horse? He's fine. He stayed with you after you must have fallen off his back. If he hadn't, I would never have seen you. You was half-buried in the snow." Mitch chuckled and moved away, leaving Reuben to stare in awe at the sky and wonder if God really had answered his prayers.

He sat huddled in a blanket, staring at the fire, hands wrapped around the tin coffee cup. Across from him Mitch casually rolled himself a cigarette and lit it with a piece of burning dried twig picked from the flames.

"What are you doing out here, Mitch?"

The cowboy chuckled again and blew out a long stream of smoke. "Why, you wishing I hadn't come looking for you?"

"No, of course not. I'm grateful. You saved my life, I reckon."

"Nice to know my efforts haven't been for nothin'. Truth be known, young fella, I am out here looking for you!"

Reuben shook his head, more in despair than anything. "Seems like a lot of people are doing that."

"Yeah ... Your pa wants to say he's sorry."

"Sorry?" Reuben blew out a blast of air as he scoffed, "My pa don't ever say sorry – not for anything!"

"Well, that may well be right, young fella, but this time he means it. He's had a change of heart, I do believe, and he wants me to take you back."

"*Back* ...?" Reuben looked away, the heat of rage causing him to break out in a sweat. "I got things to do."

"Whatever that is it'll have to wait. Mr Cole is not a man to disobey – and I need to hold onto my job."

"Lance and Henderson, they argued."

"They always argue. They're like two old washer-women, not happy unless they're squawking over something!"

"No, Mitch," Reuben turned and looked directly into the chiselled face of the cowboy, "this was more than just a squabble. Lance was wounded, wounded real bad."

"Wounded? You mean shot?"

"No. Stabbed. Deep in the chest."

"Good God Almighty!" Mitch leapt to his feet. "Who did it? Henderson?"

"It was an accident, I think ..."

"You *think*? You better get this story straight, Reuben. Your pa will be wanting a reckoning."

"That's just it, Mitch. The reckoning has already come. Lance escaped while ... Ah hell, the details don't matter. What does matter is that Lance has headed for the town of Boniface. Brown Bear may be shadowing him, but I can't be sure."

"Seems like you don't know a good deal about much, Reuben!"

"It's all ..." The pressure mounting, Reuben pounded the sides of his head with his fists. "Damn it, nothing is clear, not since I blacked out. Henderson and me, we had to hold out against those varmints who was after me. We shot 'em up real good, but Henderson, he didn't make it. Neither did poor Miles."

"Monroe? Jeez, Reuben. They're both dead?" Reuben nodded. "And Lance?"

"To the town, like I says. And the leader, a man called Banner. He did for Henderson and Monroe, I think."

"Or maybe you did?"

"Eh?"

Reuben gaped as Mitch slowly drew his pistol. "I'm taking you back, Reuben. You can explain all of this to your pa."

"No! Mitch, for pity's sake ..." In a panic, Reuben went to stand and froze as Mitch snapped back the hammer of his pistol. A dreadful, icy cloud fell across Reuben and he trembled as he fought hard to still the fear in his voice. "Mitch, listen to me – we have to go to Boniface. If Lance is there, he needs help. Medical help. And Banner, if Banner is also there ... Mitch, please, I'm begging you, let's go down to the town and find out what's what. Then I'll come back with you. I'll cause you no trouble, I give you my word."

"You're coming back with me anyways, Reuben."

"Yes, yes, I know that, Mitch, but I'm begging you. Please. You have to trust me on this. Banner, he's the reason for all of this. It was he who got those men to ride after Brown Bear. He's a murderer, Mitch, and he has to be brought to justice."

Mitch seemed to slip into deep thought. Chewing away at his bottom lip he eventually dropped his gun back into its holster. "As soon as it's done—"

"I promise you, Mitch. I'll go home with you."

This seemed to satisfy the cowboy. His eyes wandered all over their surroundings as if he were checking for something. They were camped in a slight dip, which offered them a little protection from the gnawing cold made worse by a constant breeze bringing flurries of snow across the plain. "We'll ride in nice and slow. If Lance is there, we'll find him but this Banner character ... I reckon we shoot first and ask questions later."

"That's just about how I see it, Mitch." He nodded towards the bundle of his belongings that Mitch must have placed there after finding him and bringing him here unconscious. "I'll be needing my gun if we're gonna go up against him."

Mitch gave him a look. "Gather your things and let's go."

CHAPTER TWENTY-EIGHT

B rown Bear watched from his vantage point, detached not only in distance but also emotion. Lance was barely conscious by now, the blood continuing to dribble from his wound. The women had patched him up, but only so that he would live long enough for them to hang him.

Lance sat astride an old, mangy horse, itself on its last legs. This would undoubtedly be the last duty it would ever perform. Its burden, poor, suffering Lance, looked as pale as white chalk, his red-rimmed eyes barely capable of seeing much. His head lolled onto his chest and a thin line of spittle streamed from his blue lips. He was close to death.

The gaggle of girls around him were good-natured, laughing at the man's suffering. The old bar-owner, a man the girls called Old Bill, sat on a rickety wicker chair, one hand cupped around his grizzled jaw. Along with Lance and the horse it seemed to Brown Bear that the old man would be joining them both in the grave before too long.

A larger, younger man, sporting a soiled apron, checked the knot before stepping back to admire his handy work. "That'll do I shouldn't wonder."

"Hell, do or not, let him swing," shouted out one of the girls, an enormous female with biceps that would have looked fine on a prize-fighter.

"If he drops loose," said a much prettier girl, hefting a spade in her hands, "I'll finish him by bashing his darn brains in."

"All right," said Old Bill from his chair, drawing out his Colt Dragoon. "You any last words, you worthless piece of hog swill?"

Brown Bear saw Lance's head coming up. A barely perceptible movement of his lips followed but Brown Bear was too far away to catch any words.

"What's that he said?" said Old Bill.

"He said you can go fuck yerself," cackled the big girl.

"Well, is that right?" Old Bill looked hurt, raised the gun high in the air and eased back the hammer. "Enjoy your eternity in hell, you murdering piece of filth!"

The big gun boomed, the old nag screamed, kicked, and bolted forward. With a sickening jolt, Lance dangled from the sign, kicking out with his legs, trying with every last vestige of his strength to free himself. It didn't work and soon, within a few horrible moments, he went limp, tongue protruding from a bloated, blue-veined face. The girls all shrieked in disgust as Lance, already dead, soiled himself and Old Bill laughed uproariously.

Brown Bear turned away and slinked off without a sound.

Moving stealthily to his horse, Brown Bear paused when he spotted a big man coming into the town from the far end of the street. Brown Bear dipped down out of sight and watched the man he knew only too well reining in his horse close to the livery stables. Dismounting, the man checked all-around before going up the steps to the front office.

Brown Bear waited. This would be the perfect time and place to kill this man. Reaching for the Halls he had taken from Lance's horse, he checked its load and got himself into a prone position, lining the sights towards the stables. The man responsible for all of the terrible events of the past few days wouldn't know what had hit him before he died right there, on the steps.

It was this thought that gave Brown Bear a moment's hesitation.

Why should that man have an easy death? One minute here, the next ... with no suffering, no realisation as to who had killed him? No realisation that he was dying because of what he had done? No, it was too easy. The man should know before the curtain came down on his loathsome life. In those moments of deep contemplation, the opportunity for a quick, clean kill flittered away as the man came out of the office, rubbing his chin, and stretching his back. A smaller, much older man followed him and went directly to the horse and gently led it away around back. The big man, the one Brown Bear wanted dead, moved down the street, unaware that death had hovered over him for the briefest of moments. Oblivious he walked away, Brown Bear watching him. Soon the sight of Lance swinging in the pale sunlight would reach him, then Brown Bear would act. As he should have done before. White man's business should stay White man's business, that is what Chief Two Rivers always told his people. Do not become involved in ways that you do not understand nor value, for their life is different from ours. And of less worth. Chief Two Rivers had watched his own wife shot and killed by marauding scalp hunters. He knew the wisdom of his own words to be the truth. Brown Bear should have taken more note of them. Reuben Cole had shown him that not all Whites were bad. Some were sensitive, selfless, and deserving of respect. Perhaps he owed it to Reuben to end all of this right now, while he could. Leaving his horse, he slipped into the shadows to confront his enemies and mete out justice.

CHAPTER TWENTY-NINE

As they turned into the approach to the town, a blast from a large-calibre pistol almost sent them scurrying for cover. Mitch, the first to recover, gripped Reuben's elbow as the young man went to move away. "That wasn't for us."

"Who then?"

Mitch shrugged and drew his pistol. "Best we go take a look."

The town of Saint Boniface was little more than a single street with sorry-looking wooden buildings on either side. At the end of the one side street stood a livery stable, which was a small, fenced coral and stable barely big enough for three horses. An office fronted it. Further down was a merchandise store, an assayer's office, another building which leaned horribly to the right and which was, by the sign hanging above its crooked door, a purveyor of meat. There were then several well-spaced out private dwellings and a two-storey edifice proclaiming itself as a guesthouse. Opposite ran a collection of motley looking affairs, one a dry goods store and, the most imposing, a large hotel-cum-saloon. Opposite this was the building which took all of Reuben and Mitch's attention, for swinging from its sign was the body of Lance, his neck stretched impossibly long. The sole inhabitants of this decrepit place was a collection of gaudily clad girls and a man sitting on a rickety chair gathered around, all of them laughing. And watching, a little to the side, was a large man dressed in a dark frock coat, sporting a broken-crowned top-hat.

"That's Banner," said Reuben through his teeth.

"And that there swinging is Lance."

"We're too late for him, I reckon."

Mitch blew out a sigh and slowly dismounted. "I can't leave him like that, Reuben. Let's go and introduce ourselves to that murdering bunch of cackling banshees."

Reuben took both horses and tied them to a hitching post outside a former eating establishment, now all boarded up. He turned and considered the group milling around the macabre scene. They were growing tired of their sport and were beginning to break away.

"Mitch, we need to think this through."

"I've got to help."

"Help? He's dead, Mitch. That's obvious."

"Not to me, it ain't!"

The cowboy lunged forward. Reuben made a grab for him, but Mitch swatted him away. "I'll do it alone if need be, damn you!"

"Do what for God's sake?"

"Cut him down!"

The old man and the girls traipsed into the saloon. None of them gave Reuben and Mitch so much as a glance, which gave Mitch all the edge he needed.

He stepped out into the street, gun in his hand, and shouted out, "Holdup, you bunch of swine-heads!"

They stopped, the girls in something of a fluster, the old man splitting his face into a toothless grin.

"You a friend of his, sonny?"

"You had no need to murder him like that."

"*Murder?* Is that you call the lawful hanging of that man? Were you here to witness what he did?"

"He's a murderer," said one of the girls. "He comes in here, all bleeding, and we tend to him. Then he kills poor Joshua for no reason!"

"It's justice," put in the large girl, folding her arms across her formidable bosom, "that's what it is, cowboy. Now git before I put you over my knee and spank your backside."

Reuben stepped up close to Mitch and felt the charged atmosphere growing uglier by the second. He chanced a glance behind him to see Banner slipping out of sight in the gap between an adjacent building and the store from which Lance dangled. What was he planning, Reuben wondered?

A man came out of the saloon wearing a bartender's apron. In his hands, he held a sawn-off shotgun. A mean, swarthy looking individual, Reuben had no doubts he was more than capable of using the weapon to devastating effect.

"Mitch. Let's move on."

"Wise words, for a young 'un," croaked the old man. "You can take your friend with you if you have a mind, but don't ever come back here or we'll string you up too."

The girls laughed at that and the old man seemed well pleased with himself, puffing out his chest and smacking his thin, blue lips.

"To hell with that," said Mitch who went into a half-crouch, brought up his revolver and blasted the man holding the shotgun. He flew backwards, smashed through the batwing doors, and lay there, legs twitching. Sprinting hard as the girls broke into a chorus of wild screaming, Mitch mounted the steps in a rush, grabbed hold of the shotgun, turned, and discharged both barrels into the huddle of women just as Reuben dived for cover.

By some miracle, the old man appeared unscathed while all around him, girls staggered and fell, some peppered in the face, some in the body. The noise from their broken mouths was deafening.

Reuben crouched behind a collection of wooden crates, shocked into paralysis. He could do nothing more than look on as Mitch came down the steps and fired four evenly spaced shots into the old man, blowing him around as if he were a rag on a stick in a windy day. Even before the old man crumpled, Mitch was striding across to where Reuben cowered.

"You better snap out of it, Reuben, we got work to do!"

It happened fast after that, faster than Reuben thought possible.

By now, Mitch seemed to be out of control. Ignoring the moans and groans of the stricken girls, he strode across the short stretch to where Lance's body swung so horribly from the sign. "Get yourself over here, Reuben!"

In a daze, Reuben did so.

"Hold him up, Reuben. For the love of God, hold him up, by the ankles goddammit!"

Averting his eyes, Reuben had no wish to gaze upon the bloated face of the man he'd once known. Instead, he wrapped his arms around Lance's legs and lifted him, easing the pressure of the rope.

"Damn it to hell," spat Mitch, "I don't have no knife. Hold onto him, Reuben, he's gonna drop."

A little of the feeling was returning to Reuben's body and mind. He cleared his throat. "But Mitch, how am I supposed to ..."

But before Reuben could complete his sentence, Mitch aimed his revolver. A single shot rang out and severed the hanging rope. Lance's body, a dead weight in every awful sense of the description, slumped on top of Reuben, knocking him to the ground in a heap of lifeless limbs. Screaming, Reuben scrambled out from under the dead man's body and got to his feet, arms desperately battering away at the dust and what he perceived to be pieces of Lance's dried blood from his pants and shirt.

"Will you quit doing that crazy jig," said Mitch.

"Damn it all, why didn't you warn me!"

"Will you stop hollerin'! How else was I supposed to get him down?"

"Help, we could have asked for help."

"Help? Who from, that old buzzard who I shot dead, or those whores who came at us like crazed coyotes?"

"I don't know, but you should have warned me."

"Shoot, Reuben, you need to shut your mouth. I'm about done in with your lack of respect. Lance here has left this life in a manner which he did not deserve, so you think about that for a while, eh. We'll need to get him on the back of a mule or maybe a cart and take him back to the ranch. Your pa is gonna want satisfaction for this, Reuben. I have a mind to think he may well blame you for a good deal of it."

"*Me?*" Reuben threw out his hands, "Mitch, none of this is down to me!"

"Well, none of it would have happened if you hadn't shot up those men chasing your Injun friend. That's what caused all this, I reckon."

"I agree with that."

They both jumped at the sound of this new voice. In that instant, all their disagreements vanished as they turned around to see the bulk of Banner emerging from the side of the building. His frock coat was pulled back to reveal two tied-down guns at his hips. He leaned against the store's edge, nonchalant, arrogant, a tiny smirk on his face.

"Is that him," breathed Mitch.

But Reuben was too rigid with rage and indecision to answer.

Banner, on the other hand, seemed in complete control. He pushed himself upright, sneering. "I reckon so, cowboy. And this is where it ends."

Mitch didn't hesitate. His hand flew for his gun. He was fast, taking Banner by surprise. Although the big man managed to clear his right holster, Mitch was there first, hammer engaged, barrel unwavering. "You're damn right," he said and squeezed the trigger.

Reuben learned a valuable lesson that day, one he never forgot.

In abject horror, he stared in disbelief at Mitch as the hammer fell onto an empty chamber. Mitch had not reloaded his gun. In those days, reloading a six-chambered pistol took time. The placing of powder, ball and cap relied on patience, skill, and deliberation. It was not something to be hurried or skipped. After he'd shot through the hanging rope Mitch had not bothered to reload, no doubt believing danger was no longer present. And now he was about to pay the price.

Banner blew out a loud sigh and fell back against the building, dragging a trembling hand over his face. "Damn, son, you had me dead to rights there. You sure is fast, but you have the brain of a dormouse. I thank God for it. You, boy, you unloosen your gun belt as I am thinking you is a might smarter than your friend here."

To add weight to his words, and visibly recovering his wits, Banner turned the gun on Reuben.

Mitch made a move. Reuben wanted to shout, but before he could react, Banner shot Mitch high up on the left shoulder, blowing him back across the store steps. Groaning, he rolled over onto his face. From his right hand slipped a knife, the one he had made a grab for.

"Like I said," Banner said with a sigh, "no brains."

He eased back the hammer in preparation for another shot.

The rifle rang out from somewhere across the street, but the bullet, tracing a scorching trail, hit the woodwork mere inches from Banner's head. Banner yelped and turned, visibly shaken.

Reuben, taking his chance, drew his own pistol, and fired into the bulk of the man standing before him.

Now it was Banner's turn to stagger backwards, looking down in abject horror at the widening red stain across his midriff. He stopped and turned his head towards Reuben. "Boy, I knew you weren't stupid."

"Don't call me boy," snarled Reuben and shot him again in the head.

For a moment, the only sound was the wind blowing up clouds of snow from the street. Nothing else stirred. Holstering his gun, Reuben went to Mitch and gently turned him over.

"Oh, Reuben," said the cowboy, forcing a smile. "I'm gonna bleed out."

"No, you ain't," said Reuben.

He sat down on the steps and tried to control his breathing. Knowing what had happened to Mitch, he carefully drew his gun and began to load the two empty chambers. But his hands were trembling so much he could not manage it and the gun dropped from his numbed fingers. Killing seemed to come easy to him now and he no longer recognised who he was. Mere days since, he was a gangly, happy teenager, riding out across the range, seeking out experiences to punctuate his otherwise mundane existence. Now he was a seasoned killer. And the most terrifying aspect of it all – he felt nothing. He no more considered the men shot dead by his gun than he would a cockroach crushed under his boot.

He gathered himself and climbed to his feet. There was nobody else. They were all gone to meet their maker as someone like Monroe might have said. Monroe, the only true innocent in all of this. So many lives ended. Was any of it worth it, he wondered?

Reuben bent down and picked up his gun, checked the load, and crossed to the man he'd only just shot. He stared down at Banner's lifeless body, those eyes wide open, turned towards the sky, eyes that stared bemused, bewildered. Reuben wondered who had fired the rifle but then, as he glanced up and saw the horse riding away in the distance, he knew. He should call out and thank Brown Bear, but perhaps him going his own way was for the best. The men back at the ranch would never be able to understand or accept that an Indian could ever do a good deed. He'd saved Reuben's life, gave him that edge, the only edge he needed to draw everything together and bring it to its inevitable conclusion.

Banner was dead. It was over.

CHAPTER THIRTY

He found an old sheet in the bordello and ripped off several lengths which he used to bind up Mitch's shoulder. The wounded cowboy sat in the bar, face awash with sweat, a curious sickly green colour tinting his cheeks. He held a glass of whisky in his right hand, the left now useless.

"The bullet's still in there," said Reuben. "I can dig it out, but ... Mitch, we'll ride for the ranch. We can make it by tomorrow."

Mitch nodded his head grimly.

"I should have shot him straight away," said Reuben. "If I'd done that you would not be in this—"

"Don't beat yourself up over this, Reubs. This is my fault. All of it. I should have reloaded my gun."

"I never saw anyone pull as fast as you, Mitch."

A tiny snigger escaped the cowboy's lips. "Didn't do me any good in the end, did it?"

Reuben had no answer to that. He filled up Mitch's glass. "I'm gonna find a cart or something for Lance."

"Leave him, Reuben."

Reuben stopped and gawped at his suffering companion. "Leave him? Mitch, we can't just—"

"Sure we can, Reubs. After what he did? To that girl?"

"You mean ...?" Reuben slumped down on a chair opposite.

"Yeah. Listen, I have had time to think. And this," he rolled his wounded shoulder, biting down the pain as he did so, "it's sort of cleared my head. Brought everything into focus."

"I'm not sure I understand."

"I hoped that Lance would survive. I knew there was bad feeling between him and Henderson, but if he'd lived, I could have persuaded him to come clean. It was all his fault, you see. Emily Dowers. He found out she was planning on running away with Henderson."

"*What?*"

"Don't act so shocked, Reuben. That girl ... Dear Lord, if you'd have seen her. Damn near the prettiest thing I've ever seen. And she had a way with her. A look in her eye, the pout of her mouth ... you laid eyes on her, Reuben, you wanted her in your bed, without hesitation. I've never in all my days known anything like it."

"So, you too ... " Reuben ran a hand through his hair, tugging at the roots. "But the husband, he ..."

"I reckon he brought her here from New York in the hope he would somehow be able to tame her. Never once did he consider that the men here have no propriety. We are rough and without manners. It's the nature of our work. We take what we want, without consideration. That's what happened with her and the rest of us. Me too. I lay with her. I managed to disentangle myself from her charms 'cause I always knew she was poison. It darn near broke my heart doing it, I must tell you. But Henderson ... The poor sap, he fell for her big time. And she encouraged him. Saw in him a way out."

"And when Lance caught wind of it, he killed her?"

Mitch shrugged. "Him too. He couldn't live without her. He confided in me one night when he was so drunk he didn't know what he was saying. After what the husband did."

"Mitch, I thought you said that Lance—"

"No. I said he was *responsible*. He'd gone to the cabin to have it out with her, and the husband was there. They fought and Lance put him down, as you would expect. She screamed at Lance to get out, to never come back. And as he rode off, he heard the gunshot."

"Dear God ..."

"After he'd killed her, the husband went and hanged himself. That would have been the end of it but for Henderson. He was wild with grief and Lance ... He took his time, planned his revenge."

"By planting those cigar butts in the cabin, to make it look like Henderson was the one."

"Something like that."

A sudden jolt of pain raced across his features and Mitch bent forward, clutching at his shoulder.

Reuben leapt to his feet. "Mitch, Mitch, hold on! Take the whisky, to numb the pain, and I'll go fetch the horses."

"You'd better be quick, Reubs," moaned Mitch without raising his head.

They rode through the night at a steady pace, Reuben fearful that any sudden movement might cause the bullet to move in Mitch's shoulder and cause another seizure. Mitch, slumped across his horse's neck, made the occasional groan, but apart from that, he showed little sign of discomfort. Reuben, however, knew that time was running against them and he could not afford to stop. As the dawn traced bands of pink and mauve across the sky, he longed for rest and felt certain Mitch must feel the same, but the ranch was mere hours away now. When they were within reach, Reuben would strike out and gallop towards his father's land, summon Doc Miller, get Mitch fixed up. That was the plan.

Of course, like most plans, circumstances got in the way.

Not long after the sun peeked its face above the horizon, Mitch slipped from his saddle and hit the ground hard. He remained still. Horribly still and Reuben was next to him within a heartbeat, lifting his head, about to pour water into the man's gaping, rigid mouth.

His eyes were open. Staring into nothing.

Reuben was too late.

CHAPTER THIRTY-ONE

H e didn't feel much like eating and played around with the eggs his father insisted he tried to get down.

Eventually, feeling sick, Reuben pushed the plate away and sat back. He felt his father's eyes boring into him.

"I wronged you," said his father after a long pause. "I wronged you and I'm sorry."

Bringing his face up, Reuben considered his father's grizzled features. He'd aged these past days, the weight of stress and anxiety taking their toll. He also knew how difficult it was for a man such as he was to offer an apology. Proud, uncompromising, certain of his unswerving righteousness, Reuben could think of no other time that his father had ever shown remorse, regret or, in this instance, admission of a mistake. But here it was, and he welcomed it, despite the anger developing inside him.

With the loss of his father's top men – Lance, Henderson, and Mitch – Reuben had been offered the job of foreman but of course, he'd refused. He was too young. The ranch needed a man of experience, of honour, a man to be respected.

"It's gonna be hard to find anyone like that," his father said, gazing at the tabletop, his face serious, laced with concern. "News from out

East is bad, Reuben. Seems like Secessionists from South Carolina have attacked a fort, bombarding it with canons and forcing its surrender."

"What does that mean, Pa?"

"It means the President will react and enforce the rule of law upon that State. Which can only mean one thing."

"War? But how can one State stand up to the forces of the country?"

"They can't, but I have heard rumours that more states will join South Carolina, form their own government and break away. Secede. Lincoln won't allow that."

"I don't understand none of it, Pa."

"I take on board what you said, Reuben, about your lack of experience and all but these are peculiar times, and I can't see we have much choice."

"How's about I ride over to Fort Defiance and canvas for a new foreman? It could be I strike lucky."

"You sure you feel up to it?"

"I think it'll be the best way of getting all that has happened out of my darn head, Pa."

"You could be right, but Fort Defiance? That's where all this started. What if that Banner has some friends there?"

"I doubt it."

"But what if he has?"

"Then I'll deal with it. Pa, if you have the confidence in me being foreman here, giving out orders to men who have worked on the range all their lives, then you have to believe I can look after myself against some dull-witted gunhands."

"If they are dim-witted."

"I reckon they are, given what I know about the men who rode with Banner. He'd have chosen the best of 'em and by God, Pa, they were not the best of anything!"

"Don't cuss, Reuben."

"Yes. Sorry, Pa."

His father gnawed away at his bottom lip for a few moments, lost in thought. Then, with sudden resolve, he slapped the tabletop with both hands. "Yes, by golly. Go there and choose a good man, Reuben. Use every ounce of those wits that have got you through all of this. Bring back a good 'un."

Beaming, Reuben got to his feet, gave a small nod, and went to get himself ready.

The weather was clear and crisp, the snowstorms over, the rolling landscape a white blanket but no longer treacherous under hoof as he rode, scarf across his mouth, fur-lined collar pulled up around his throat.

In the late afternoon, he reined in his horse. Fort Defiance nestled in the dip some thirty minutes or so away. Without turning, he took a breath and spoke. "Didn't think I'd see you again for a while."

Chuckling, Brown Bear came up next to him. "You're good, my young friend."

"You shouldn't have left the way you did. Not from the cabin, not from that damn town."

"I had little choice. They would have brought me back to your father's place and lynched me, as they tried before."

"No. I would have—"

"You could not have stopped them a second time."

"But you hadn't done anything!"

"You think such details matter to men like that?" Shaking his head, he looked down towards the fort. "Those men, the one called Banner, they delighted in causing me pain. Such things will never end, my friend. There will always be men such as those wherever I or others of my people go."

"Things might change, my friend. There's gonna be a war, Pa said. A war to free the slaves."

"Will that bring freedom, you think?"

"I ..." Reuben frowned, shrugged, and looked away. "I'm not even sure what freedom means. The right to do and say what you want I reckon. No matter your skin colour. That's what Pa says, and I agree with him."

"Even if what you want is to kill others because they are not like you? No, Reuben, it is best if I stay away, distant, in the shadows, until this trouble you say is coming is over."

"More than just trouble, I reckon."

"Then, until we meet again ..."

Reuben turned and stretched out his hand. Brown Bear took it. "Thank you," said Reuben.

"It was a way to pay my debt towards you, my friend. But it is a debt that has not yet been repaid in full."

Before Reuben could reply, Brown Bear pulled his horse away and kicked it into a full gallop.

Reuben watched his friend disappear into the distance until he was nothing more than a grey smudge on the fields of pure white.

There were soldiers at the fort. As Reuben reined in his horse, he looked around him. Blue-clad men mingled amongst the many rough-looking types spilling out of the saloon. There was lots of laughter and back-slapping and Reuben watched and wondered what was happening. He dismounted and almost immediately, a large, strong hand clamped around his shoulder. He instinctively reached for his gun, but the owner of the hand, a huge, cheery faced soldier sporting sergeant stripes on both arms, merely laughed.

"Hold on there, young fella, I mean you no harm."

"Sorry," said Reuben, relaxing a little.

"What you doing here? If you're looking for a good time, the fort will be closing its doors before long. That's why we're here. Company D, 10th Infantry Regiment, United States Army. These men you see all around you, they are drifters, would-be prospectors, chancers. We're offering 'em the chance to serve, make something of their otherwise miserable lives."

"To serve?"

"Yes. To enlist in the United States Army. We could use young men of calibre, of skill. I see by your apparel you are not a drifter."

"My name is Reuben Cole. I'm a range-boss for my father's ranch."

The soldier blew out a silent whistle. "So, you're well accustomed to tending to horses and cattle?"

"I'm a tracker."

Reuben saw the man's expression change, from one of nonchalant interest to complete attention. "A *tracker*?"

Reuben nodded. It was a lie, but perhaps not such a great one. Brown Bear had shown him so much and some of it he had already put to good use.

"This gets better and better! Seems like providence is upon us, my good young fella. How do you feel joining us as an Army tracker?"

"I'd say that would be a mighty fine thing, sir."

The sergeant's beaming grin grew broader, and he clapped that huge hand across Reuben's shoulder, almost knocking him off balance.

"I'd have to inform my father, mind. He sent me here to recruit men to help him out at the ranch. We've had some trouble, you see. We require replacements."

"Well, we can do what we can, but we have been ordered to move fast. Armies are massing, young fella, and we have little time to spare."

"I should get word to him."

"Then we will. There is one thing. You look a tad young, pardon me for saying so. But how old are you?"

Without hesitation, Reuben uttered another lie, "I'm nineteen next month."

And with that Reuben was recruited into the United States Army as a scout.

Soon, hostilities would become more than rumour and Reuben's formative years were to aid him to develop into a hardened man of action.

The end of this first instalment of Reuben Cole's early days.

Dear reader,

We hope you enjoyed reading *Born To Track*. Please take a moment to leave a review, even if it's a short one. Your opinion is important to us.

Discover more books by Stuart G. Yates at https://www.nextchapter. pub/authors/stuart-g-yates

Want to know when one of our books is free or discounted? Join the newsletter at http://eepurl.com/bqqB3H

Best regards,
Stuart G. Yates and the Next Chapter Team

Lightning Source UK Ltd.
Milton Keynes UK
UKHW040625050521
383143UK00010B/165/J

9 781034 784848